I0677473

13 BODIES

SEVEN TALES OF MURDER & MADNESS

OTHER BOOKS BY THOM REESE

THE DEMON BAQASH
CHASING KELVIN
DEAD MAN'S FIRE

13 BODIES

SEVEN TALES OF MURDER & MADNESS

THOM REESE

SPEAKING VOLUMES, LLC

NAPLES, FLORIDA

2011

13 BODIES - *SEVEN TALES OF MURDER & MADNESS*

Copyright © 2011 by THOM REESE

All rights reserved. No part of this book may be reproduced or transmitted in any form or by any means without written permission of the author.

ISBN 978-1-61232-003-8

Library of Congress Control Number: 2010942880

A NOTE FROM THE AUTHOR

The stories in this collection had their first incarnation as audio dramas. I'd written each for my radio show, 21st CENTURY AUDIO THEATRE, back in 2007 and 2008 and these were later published, in 2010, by SPEAKING VOLUMES QUALITY AUDIO BOOKS. When Kurt Mueller from SPEAKING VOLUMES approached me about doing short story adaptations I became excited. Here was a chance to flesh out these yarns in a way that could not be done in a twenty-three minute audio drama. Here was an opportunity to get inside my character's heads, to explore emotions and motivations, tell the story behind the story.

It's been a fun process, a challenging process. The stories, for the most part, have remained true to their origins, though, in some instances, I've taken some artistic liberty in order to give a fuller accounting of the events recorded. As well, some details have been changed or augmented to better fit the more intimate medium of a written narrative. As a writer, it's an interesting experience to revisit one's work after a span of years. I was able to view these tales through fresh eyes, to envision new and intriguing details, to bring a new energy to the project.

I'd be remiss if I didn't thank the many talented voice actors who lent their skills to 21st CENTURY AUDIO THEATRE. In particular those who were involved on a regular basis: Jeff Granstrom, Ken Chapman, Jan Baker, Phil Smith, Jill Martin, Tanja Montez. As well, my wife Kathy deserves a huge thank you. Not only did she co-produce the show, engineer it, and compose original music for every episode, but she is my most helpful – and critical – reader, catching all of my little writing and plotting blunders and helping to keep me on track. I'd also like to thank Gaylon Kent for his feedback on several of these short stories, and, of course, Kurt at SPEAKING VOLUMES

Table of Contents

TWO SONS

Tony Russell tapped the "end call" button and silently stared at the lifeless plastic device in his palm. How he longed to hurl the thing against the nearest wall, to stomp on it, to destroy it the way his life had been destroyed.

Instead, he calmly slid it into his pocket, breathed deeply, and tried to slip into the mask of a normal, well-adjusted human being.

"Tony, who was it?"

Great. Shirley had heard him take the call. The last thing he needed right now was to talk about this further. It was difficult enough trying to keep his own emotions in check, much less providing his wife a shoulder to cry on. It wasn't that he was unsympathetic to her, there was simply nothing left to give. It would be better, he thought, if she'd just pop another antidepressant and ignore him altogether.

Tony turned toward his wife of seven years. Her once lustrous hair was dull and lifeless. Streaks of gray had appeared along her hairline. Her face was drawn and weary, her eyes sunken. She was only twenty-seven, but suddenly seemed forty. Certainly these past few weeks had aged him as well, probably into his sixties or beyond. How were they expected to function?

Forget function, how were they even to survive?

Tony did not move toward his wife, but lingered in his current position, allowing the space between them to remain, perhaps even to expand. "It was Paul Bullard, honey. A key witness, Ricky Davies, reversed his testimony, probably due to gang threats. Jacko Singleton was released. Not enough evidence to hold him."

Shirley's once-angelic face took on the countenance of sheer horror. "But, he killed Charlie."

Still, Tony did not move to comfort the woman he loved. "I know, Shirley. Paul's working on it. He says…"

"Charlie was only six. He was just a baby."

Tony remained still, silent. What could he offer to her when he was himself an empty husk?

Now, she was building toward hysteria. "It was just a stray bullet! It wasn't even meant for him. He was just standing... He was only six!"

"Paul says that maybe we can..."

"Drive by shooting! My boy is dead! He had nothing to do with that gang war. He should be alive right now!"

Enough.

Tony couldn't take much more of this. Shirley didn't need to scream at him. Every day, every hour. Screaming. Crying. Didn't she get it? Didn't she understand that his soul had died with that child, that he was black inside? Didn't she understand that she was married to a corpse? Moving quickly toward his wife, fists clenched, Tony bellowed, "He was my boy too!"

"Then what are you going to do about it?"

Tony turned away, fought the urge to lash out, to strike, to further damage the only relationship left to him. He breathed, flexed his fingers, sought to calm himself. "Paul's working on other witnesses," he said in a near even tone. "He's our lawyer."

"I didn't ask what Paul was going to do. I asked what you're going to do."

Tony turned left, then right. He moved as if to make the door, and then redirected toward the kitchen. He could rarely stand still, but had to keep moving, keep busy, anything, just... Anything. "I don't know, Shirley. I really don't know." His voice was a sub-zero calm, but the turmoil within continued to boil.

It was several moments before Shirley again spoke, but when she did, her voice was even, unemotional, barely recognizable as someone he knew and loved. "Well, you'd better figure it out, Tony. That's all I have to say. You'd better figure it out."

And then she left Tony alone in the room.

*****

The next morning Tony sat in his office cubicle staring at his Dell. For how long, he didn't know. Concentration was an elusive thing these days.

And as to debits and credits, did any of that really matter anymore? Did one single thing in life mean anything at all? If his boss, Gene Henderson, fired him today, would it matter? If Tony stepped out in front of a speeding semi-truck, would it matter? Did anything matter even in the slightest?

He sincerely doubted it.

Tony was brought out of his brood by the sound of someone repeating his name. He glanced up to see Gene Henderson standing over him, a manila folder clutched between calloused fingers, a worried look in his sea blue eyes. "You okay, Tony?"

Tony shrugged. How does a guy answer a stupid question like that?

Henderson nodded. At least at some level he understood. "Listen," he said. "I know you're not a drinker, but you're going through hell right now. Ann, Lou, and I are headed to Clancy's Pub after work. I thought maybe you could use one. You know, take the edge off."

Tony nodded. Henderson was an okay guy. He was trying at least. "No thanks. I appreciate it, but Shirley needs me at home."

Henderson nodded. He got it. "Listen, if there's anything I can do – anything – you let me know. I'm serious. Don't be afraid to ask."

"No. Nothing you can do." Tony paused, cocked his head, offered a faux smile. "Not unless you've got a gun you want to loan me."

Henderson's face dropped. It seemed the color might have fled him.

"Just gallows humor, Gene. Blowing off some steam. Nothing to worry about." Tony turned back toward his computer monitor. "Go have a drink for me. Have some fun. I'll be fine."

"Really?"

No. Of course not, really.

"Yes, really. I just need some space. You know, some time to think about what comes next."

Gene nodded, patted Tony on the back, and walked away. He was an okay guy.

*****

There he was. That little sleaze that killed Charlie. Just hanging out, laughing, screwing around as if he was some normal guy. Charlie was dead because of him. He'd never grow up. Never have a girlfriend. Never have a life. Why did this hoodlum get to live when Charlie rotted in a grave? What made this worm so charmed? Why couldn't Jacko Singleton die? Why couldn't it have been him? No one would miss him. No one. Some people might even applaud if there was one less gang-banger on the streets. Clean up the trash. That's what it was. Cleaning up the trash. Shirley had asked Tony what he was going to do. What she'd really meant was what would he do about Jacko Singleton? What was he willing to do to set things right?

Tony put the car into gear, glared at the scumbag one last time, and then pulled away.

What to do about Jacko Singleton?

*****

"Tony, you've barely touched your dinner."

Tony glanced up at Shirley and then down at his plate. "I guess I'm not in a hungry kind of mood."

"I'm getting worried about you."

Tony slammed his fist on the table. What kind of an idiot was she? "Don't push me, Shirley. Don't..." He saw her then. Really saw her. Saw the hurt in her eyes, the emerging lines on her face. They shared an agony. Why was he being so selfish as to suppose that he alone carried the weight? "I'm sorry, honey. I'm..." he trailed off. There really wasn't any need to explain.

There was an awkward silence. Shirley slipped a forkful of peas into her mouth, chewed, swallowed, and then said, "You were late again today."

Tony stared down at his plate. No eye contact, no connection. "Yeah. I was late."

"Where were you?"

Tony stared past his wife to the stove. Dingy. Grease-splattered. There was a bundle of bananas sitting beside it. Brown, nearly black. Shirley might have purchased them as a snack for Charlie all those weeks ago. After several moments, he returned his gaze to Shirley. "Like I said, I was late."

Shirley loaded some more peas onto her fork and then asked tentatively, "Would you like some mashed potatoes?"

Again, Tony's fist slammed onto the table. The silverware jumped. Peas tumbled from Shirley's fork. "I told you already. I'm not hungry!"

Tony was up and away from the table. He didn't know where he was going, couldn't even contemplate his next move, but he couldn't just sit around waiting for something to happen. That was the one thing he couldn't do.

*****

There he was again – the punk, the thug. Charlie's killer. What was that? Weed? Hey, maybe he'd even score some crack. Maybe some meth. Wouldn't it be something if Jacko Singleton overdosed? It would be poetic, in a way. The killer killed by his own stupidity. But, it wouldn't be that simple. Nothing was that simple. Singleton thought he was charmed. Thought he was Teflon. He thought he'd live forever. Well, no one lived forever. No one. Something would bring Jacko Singleton down. Something or someone.

Tony depressed the accelerator, allowing the engine to roar. Singleton looked his way, perhaps fearing that he was about to be run down.

Yeah, a little fear in his life. That's what the punk needed, a little healthy fear.

Easing off the gas, Tony put the Chevy Malibu into gear, rolled slowly in Singleton's direction, and then turned the corner onto Fifth Street.

Not today, Jacko.

Not today.

But, soon.

*****

The scream pierced the night as it did most nights. Tony sat bolt upright, the sheets covered in sweat, his limbs quivering uncontrollably. Shirley was there of course. Shirley was always there, trying to comfort him, telling him that things would one day be alright, that they would somehow survive this. But, nothing would be alright – not ever. And Shirley knew this too. It was evident in her thinning face, in her distant stare, in her increasing dependence on antidepressants. She no longer wore make-up. She rarely even showered. And worse yet, Tony had nothing to offer her. No consolation. No comfort. No hope. He found it a profound effort to offer a simple hug. She was trying. He could see that. She was trying to reach out to him. But, all he could think of was that one question she had posed. What was he going to do? What was he going to do about Jacko Singleton?

*****

It was three weeks after Shirley had posed the dreadful question that Tony approached Gene Henderson. The man was squinting at his computer monitor, examining an Excel spreadsheet and didn't notice Tony's presence until he spoke. "Gene, you have a moment?"

Henderson turned, glanced up, and offered a smile. A genuine smile. A warm, welcoming grin that nearly made Tony turn away in shame. Henderson wasn't a bad guy. Not a bad guy at all. Tony felt awful for deceiving him. "Oh, Tony," he said. "How are you doing today?"

"A little better, thanks." Tony hesitated, shoved his hands in his pockets, gazed at his feet. "Um, I really need to apologize. I've been a jerk lately."

Henderson rose, and then patted Tony on the shoulder, his glassy blue eyes emitting compassion, his touch, sincerity. "Tony, don't apologize. It's amazing you've held together at all."

Tony nodded. "Listen, I've slipped behind on some of my work. You know, trouble concentrating. I think I'm going to take my laptop and hibernate in the conference room for a couple of hours. You know, away from all of the noise and distractions."

"Sure, Tony. That's fine. You just do what you've got to do."

"You know, Gene, that's exactly what I intend to do."

*****

It was hot, muggy; Tony's shirt stuck to his skin as heat simultaneously beat down from above and radiated upward from the old and cracked asphalt. Jacko Singleton was apparently completing a drug deal. Tony saw money exchange hands and then two fists pressing each other in lieu of a handshake. Singleton turned, making his way down an alleyway – just as Tony knew he would. Tony knew Singleton's routines, knew just how the scumbag lived. He'd studied him, followed him. And right now, for these few moments, Singleton was alone. All alone.

Tony emerged from behind a corner. "Hey, Jacko."

The punk turned. Maybe a bit nervously, but still he affected a false confidence. "Who are you?"

Tony took a step forward. "What do you mean, who am I?"

The young punk cocked his head, narrowed his eyes, and stood legs spread wide, arms crossed at the chest. The posture of a tough guy. "You lookin' to buy?"

"Am I looking to buy? You have no idea who I am, do you?"

"Listen, Mister. You don't want no trouble. I got friends who…"

"You've got friends? I think you take care of yourself pretty well on your own – Jacko." Tony moved forward, nearly breathing in the kid's face. "Don't you have any idea who I am?"

Singleton shook his head. Was that fear? God, this street tough looked like a frightened twelve year-old. He wasn't twelve. Tony knew this. He was sixteen, old enough to be charged as an adult, if the crime was murder.

"You sat in the courtroom with me every day for a week and you don't know who I am? You killed my son and you don't know who I am?"

The kid's eyes went wide. The cocky street kid was gone, replaced by what? A terrified youngster?

No.

Not a kid. Nothing innocent. Nothing pure.

This punk was scum. Nothing but murdering scum.

"What do you want?" stammered the scum. "I didn't do nothin'."

"What do I want? I want my son back, you little worm."

Singleton gazed up at Tony, his mouth agape, his fingers fidgeting. "I told you in the courtroom, I didn't kill your son."

The gun was in Tony's hand now: heavy, cold, unfamiliar.

"No, man. I didn't do nothin'. Honest. It wasn't me."

Was that urine? Did Tony smell urine? Had this kid actually peed his pants?

Tony raised the gun. It seemed to grow heavier yet. Singleton turned to run. Tony squeezed. The explosion from within the chamber was deafening. Singleton tumbled to the ground, an open bag of M & M's spilling from his grasp and onto the hot asphalt.

The gun was heavy. Far too heavy.

*****

It was just after six pm when the doorbell rang. Shirley sat alone at the kitchen table eating microwaveable White Castle hamburgers while Tony sat rigid on the living room couch staring at his neglected twenty gallon aquarium. Three of the formerly seven inhabitants of the tank remained. Certainly, these would soon join their former companions in the city sewer system.

The detective was a jowly man with horn rimmed glasses, rolled up shirt sleeves, and basset hound eyes. He stared up at Tony as the door swung open. "Anthony Russell?"

"I'm Tony Russell. Who are you?"

The shorter man offered a business card. "Mr. Russell, I'm Detective Wes Dolton. May I come inside?"

Tony hesitated. His right hand offered an involuntary twitch. His stomach contracted. It had been four days since the shooting. Four long torturous days. Finally, just within the past hour, Tony had begun to think that perhaps he'd actually gotten away with it, that somehow he'd pulled this thing off. What was it they always said in detective novels, if they don't find the killer within the first twenty-four hours, chances were they never would?

Had there been a witness?

No. If there had been, the detective would have shown up much sooner. Besides, if Tony was to be arrested, uniformed officers would surely be present.

"Mr. Russell?"

"Oh, uh, yeah. Come in. Does this have something to do with my son's murder?"

Dolton nodded as he crossed the threshold into the small, dimly lit living area. "In a way, yes. There have been a couple of new developments in the case."

Tony led Dolton to the couch and offered him a seat. Tony sat on a threadbare recliner opposite the detective. "Did they finally bring Jacko Singleton back in?" asked Tony.

Dolton seemed to survey the place, taking in the family photos on the walls, noting the ill-kept aquarium, glancing into the cluttered kitchen where Shirley remained, seemingly unaware of the visitor, chomping on her White Castles and thumbing through a three month old People magazine. Her physician had put her on a new antidepressant, but the thing left her listless and uninterested. Either that, or it was just plain ineffective and Shirley was spiraling deeper yet. Tony found it increasingly difficult to care one way or the other.

"Yesterday morning, Singleton was found in a dumpster, dead," said Dolton. "He'd been there at least three days."

Tony shifted in his seat and focused on a photograph of Charlie hanging just behind and to the right of Dolton's head. "Well, wow. Uh, you have to know that's good news to me."

"I understand that, Mr. Russell. But, like I said, there have been a *couple* of developments."

Tony readjusted again. It seemed he couldn't quite figure out what to do with his hands: fold them together, clasp the arm rest, cross his arms? "Meaning what exactly?" he asked finally choosing to clasp them before him in his lap.

"Another gang member has been implemented in the death of your son. There's evidence pointing to this suspect. In all likelihood, Mr. Russell, we've found your son's killer."

No, no, no. This wasn't right. This man had to be tossing out false information, looking for a reaction, seeing if Tony would implicate himself. Tony crossed his legs, tried to appear calm, nearly uninterested. "But, they were so certain it was Jacko Singleton."

The detective's droopy eyes were clear, bright. His expressionless face knowing. He knew! The man already knew. Tony glanced at Shirley. She'd angled her head in his direction, but had yet to say anything. Maybe she was in on it too. Maybe she'd figured everything out, called the police.

"Everything happened quickly, Mr. Russell. Singleton was in the car during the drive-by, but he wasn't the shooter. We have solid evidence this time."

This was bull!

This detective, this Dolton, he was throwing out a bunch of bull, tricking Tony, trying to trip him up.

"Well, um, that's good – right? I mean, we need to get this behind us. You know, move on."

"I'm sure you do, Mr. Russell." The man paused, his moist brown eyes glassy in the dim light.

Glassy, but knowing.

Penetrating.

It felt as if the man was reaching down into Tony's very soul itself.

"Listen," added Dolton as he leaned forward, elbows resting casually on his upper thighs. "I'm sorry to have to ask you this, but regarding Jacko Singleton, we now need to solve his murder. You obviously had motive. Do you mind answering a few questions so we can eliminate you as a suspect?"

Tony glanced at Shirley as she flipped another page – uninterested, uncaring.

"Uh, sure, Detective. I understand."

"I'll try to make this brief. Where were you on this past Tuesday afternoon between the hours of two and four?"

Shirley flipped another page. It seemed her head nodded listlessly. Her eyes fluttered. How could she pretend not to know what was happening?

"At work. I was at work. Templeton Administrative Services."

"And someone can corroborate this?"

"Uh, yeah. My boss. Gene Henderson."

Dolton nodded. Why wasn't he taking notes? Maybe because he already knew. He was just playing the game, waiting for Tony to trip up.

"Do you own a handgun, Mr. Russell?"

"No, no. I've never owned a gun."

Shirley was looking in this direction now, her expression dreamy, yet still, something in her expression – curiosity, guile, mirth? What did she know? What was she keeping from him?

"When was the last time you saw Jacko Singleton?"

Tony shifted in his seat, glanced down at his stocking feet. Why hadn't he put shoes on before the detective arrived? He was sitting here in his stockings!

"I guess that would have been three weeks ago, in the courtroom."

"Not since then?"

Why would he ask that same question a second time? Shirley was facing them now, her face showing concern. What had she done? Had she called this man? Had she brought this trouble to their home?

"Listen, Detective," Tony tried to sound calm. He even forced something akin to a smile. "Singleton was a thug. If he didn't kill my boy, then he was probably going to kill someone else eventually. Aren't we better off without him?"

"Well, that's not how his mother sees it, Mr. Russell."

The detective remained for nearly another twenty minutes, asking Tony another handful of useless – but leading – questions, and then moving on to Shirley, who seemed listless and disconnected. The detective showed some concern at this and, before leaving, pulled Tony aside, suggesting he keep an eye on his wife. Obviously, she was over-medicated, probably taking more than the recommended dosage. She was depressed, having lost a son, and prone to irrational behavior. At this last statement, Dolton's eyes had locked with Tony. Yes, Tony knew about irrational behavior, he knew all too well about irrational behavior. The problem was, some irrational actions couldn't be reversed.

*****

Three days later there was a gang killing. The next day, another. Two more the following day. According to news reports, police believed that the slaying of Jacko Singleton had ignited a wave of retaliation killings between two gangs. Singleton's mother appeared on the news, pleading for an end to the violence, asking for a spirit of forgiveness.

Forgiveness.

Was there even such a thing?

Had Singleton's death really sparked this wave of violence? Was Tony ultimately responsible for all of these deaths?

Tony began scanning the news sites online, searching for information of the Singleton investigation, but even more so, devouring scraps and tidbits on the increased gang violence. This couldn't be his fault. He couldn't be responsible.

And even if, in some insane universe, he had ignited the fire, Singleton was a beast. Plain. Simple. None of this mattered. They were all beasts. All of them. Not kids. Not innocents, despite their young ages. These were murdering scum. And they were doing what murdering scum did. It was one of these that took Charlie from him.

One of these but not any of these.

Night after night, Tony stared at the aquarium. Only one fish remained. He glanced into the kitchen, three day old dishes in the sink, potato peels littering the floor about the circular trash can. There sat Shirley amidst the mess, gazing vacantly at the same worn out magazine. He ran his fingers through his hair. Greasy. When had he last washed it? It didn't matter, he supposed. Nothing mattered any more.

And everything mattered.

He lifted his knees nearly to his chest, curling into a ball at the edge of the couch. Was that fish dead? That final fish. Was it bobbing upside-down in the tank? Tony's hair was greasy. Shirley sat in the kitchen. The fish bobbed. Tony's hair was greasy. Shirley sat in the kitchen. The fish bobbed. Tony's hair was greasy…

*****

The police station seemed frenzied. Phones rang, officers marched one way and then another, a woman sat in a corner crying, a man yelled at a female detective, pounded on her desk, inundated her with profanities. Tony glanced one direction and then another, half expecting someone to point, to identify him as a killer, a murderer. But he was invisible. Even Dolton barely noticed him as he approached the man's desk. Tony considered turning around, racing from the room, climbing into his car and driving far, far away. If asked, he couldn't have explained why he'd come here, what misguided purpose had drawn him away from work midday and pushed him into this room. Pulse racing, hands clammy, Tony glanced about, seeking an exit sign, an adjacent hallway, anything. But, just as he hesitated, just as he thought to veer left and avoid the detective, Dolton glanced up, an expression of half recognition in his rheumy brown eyes.

"Detective Dolton, I'm Tony Russell. Charlie Russell's father." Tony was seated before he'd even consciously decided to approach the man.

Dolton sipped from a severely chipped – nearly dangerous looking – mug and then nodded. "I remember you, Mr. Russell. What can I do for you?"

Tony shifted slightly to his right and then crossed his legs. "Well, nothing really."

He paused, adding nothing. The detective merely took another sip of java as he waited for Tony to continue.

"What I mean is, Jacko Singleton, his murder; all of these other gang murders, they're not really all because of Jacko's killing. The media's sensationalizing – right? These gang members, they'd be killing each other even if Singleton was still alive."

Another sip of java. A weary stare through liquid eyes. "What's that to you, Mr. Russell? If I remember correctly, you think all of these gang members are subhuman. We're better off without them."

"Well, no. Not exactly."

Dolton set his cup aside and stared at Tony through scratched and scuffed lenses. "What are you trying to say, Mr. Russell?"

Coming here had been a mistake. Why was Dolton staring at Tony like that? Why didn't he tell Tony what he really thought, what he really suspected? "All of these deaths," said Tony after a pause. "It seems such a waste. I mean, are you sure that Jacko Singleton didn't kill my boy?"

"Yes, sir. We are now sure of that."

"And all of these other murders?"

"They started as retaliation for the Singleton murder. His gang, the Blood Brotherhood, assumed Singleton's death to be at the hand of another gang, the Tribe. The Brotherhood swore to kill two of the Tribe in retaliation. The Tribe then announced that they would kill two Brotherhood members for every Tribe member slain. It just kept going from there."

Tony stood. He pivoted left, having convinced himself to leave. There was nothing for him here. Every moment buried him deeper. Turning once again toward Dolton, he said, "But, they're gang members. They're always killing each other anyway. Right?"

Dolton leaned back in his chair, sipped another nip of java, and contemplated Tony for several seconds. "Mr. Russell, is there something you want to tell me?"

"No... I just... I thought... I just came down here to thank you for catching my son's killer. That's all."

With that, Tony Russell turned and marched from the office. Not until he was safely in his car and on the road was he certain that no one had followed him with the purpose of arresting him.

*****

Tony almost never drank alcohol. He'd spent most of his adult life a church-going man, and as such, he had a church-going man's sensibilities. No, he didn't think alcohol was evil – not entirely – but it certainly brought about more ills in society than benefits. And as for his own life, truly, what was the need? People claimed the stuff rid a man of inhibitions, allowed him to be his true self. But, wasn't it true that those inhibitions are a part of the true self, that when one suppresses a portion of his natural being, that what is left is less of who that person truly is, not more? That what one is really left with is the baser part of a man not the better? Truly, what the drink has suppressed is the part that makes a man civilized, the element that separates him from the beasts of the world. Then again, Tony had proven that he could be very well the beast while entirely sober.

Despite his better judgment, despite his natural aversion to the stuff, Tony had decided to stop by a local bar and ingest the bitter liquid. His life had already crumbled, what greater harm was there to be done? Nothing could ever be as it had been; Tony could never again be whole, why not dilute his true self further yet? Even more to the point, Tony simply could no longer tolerate his own company. When he thought of what he'd done…

What he'd done!

How could he have allowed Shirley to push him into such a thing? No, she hadn't actually told him to kill Singleton, had never uttered such a word, but that had been implicit in her goading question. "What are you going to do? What are you going to do about it?" she had asked. It had to have been what she'd meant. It had to. Tony sipped his fifth beer and stared at his watch. The workday would be almost over. He should call Shirley; tell her he wouldn't be home on time. Maybe tell her that they were done. That he could never forgive her for what she'd made him do. Tell her that he truly hated her, that she could sit there staring at her People magazine and popping her antidepressants for the rest of her days for all he cared. Maybe that was exactly what he should do.

It took four attempts to accurately dial the number on his iPhone. Five beers may not seem much to an established drinker, but to Tony it was enough to significantly impair. When finally he'd succeeded in making the call, when after three rings Shirley had answered, her voice was dreamy, far away. "Tony?"

"Shirley. I'm so sorry."

"Tony, what is it? Are you alright?"

Why was it that now that he heard her voice he loved her again? How was it that when he was alone in his thoughts all he wanted to do was scream at her, to curse her into eternity for what she'd made him do? But when he heard her voice, that certain timbre, that subtle lilt, that then he longed to hold her until his very last breath?

"Tony, I've been worried. Gene Henderson called. He said you hadn't been to work in three days. He said that that detective came by, asking if you'd been at work when the Singleton boy was killed."

How could she seem so surprised? How could she even question his deeds or motives? She'd been the instigator. She'd pushed him to this. If she'd had any backbone at all, she would have pulled the trigger herself instead of damning Tony to everlasting guilt and despair. "You wanted me to do something, Shirley. You asked me what I was going to do. But, I didn't know what to do. I hurt so bad. Honey, I hurt so bad."

"Tony, where are you? It sounds like you've been drinking." Shirley's words were slow, deliberate. Obviously, she was battling with her medication, trying to get the upper hand.

"I thought you wanted me to do something. To take action. Shirley, all those kids are dead. All those kids." Tony was weeping openly, blubbering, actually. The bartender glanced toward his booth, but then returned to cleaning a glass. Certainly, a weeping drunk was nothing new. Tony wasn't concerned that the man heard his words. What did it matter who heard him now? What did anything matter?

"Tony, please. Tell me what it is you're trying not to say." Her voice was stronger now. Perhaps the conversation had momentarily shocked her from her stupor.

"Your father's Colt, you remember it?"

"The heirloom? The gun from World War One? Tony, what did you do?"

*****

Somehow, two hours later, he found himself at Althea Singleton's door. Jacko's home. At first, the slain boy's mother did not answer the door. It was the kind of neighborhood where doors were rarely answered, where crimes were rarely reported. But Tony persisted, ringing the bell over and over, knocking, calling out to her. Finally, when he'd identified himself as Charlie Russell's father, the metal screen door swung open with a regretful clank and rattle. "Mr. Russell, what is it you want?"

Her eyes were of the deepest brown. And they knew sorrow. Oh, how they knew sorrow. The sorrow that only those who have lost a child could know. Tony was still feeling the effects of the alcohol, but managed to straighten himself, to look her directly in the eye. Why had he come? What had he hoped to accomplish through this encounter?

Did he want her forgiveness?

No. That he didn't deserve. Perhaps a shared sorrow, the comfort of one who shared a common grief.

"Mr. Russell," she repeated. "Why are you here?"

"We both lost sons, Mrs. Singleton. Both of us. I'm just…" He didn't know what to say, how to finish the sentence. They shared a loss, yes. But where his loss was only marginally connected to her, he was the direct cause of her pain. How could he ever hope to share anything with this poor woman? He was the devil incarnate. He was the instrument of her misery. He glanced at the ground, pursed his lips, breathed once, twice. And then, taking one long breath, he continued. "I'm sorry for your loss, Ma'am. I… I'm sorry…"

He couldn't say it. He couldn't force the confession from his lips. The tears got in the way, crowding out all else. And so he reached behind himself to where he'd lodged the heirloom in his belt. Right at the base of his spine. He had not planned this final act. Not consciously at least. Though, he had brought the weapon, he had kept it on his person. Perhaps this had subconsciously been the plan all along. He would never know for sure.

Althea Singleton's eyes grew wide as Tony withdrew the long barreled Colt. But whether out of paralyzing shock or of an unnatural understanding as to his intent, she did not scream, nor did she flee.

"I'm sorry, Mrs. Singleton. I'm so sorry about your boy."

Slowly, so very slowly, Tony inserted the gun into his mouth, slipping it between his lips, tasting the slick gun oil with his tongue. The barrel was cold, much colder than he'd anticipated. It clicked against two of his teeth causing minor pain. On another day he might have complained of this. He breathed twice deeply, and then squeezed the trigger. Nothing happened. Perhaps he hadn't really squeezed at all. But, this time. This time he'd squeeze just a little bit harder, just a bit more pressure from the...

FAMILY LEGACY

Having concern that common mud might be used with murderous intent could be considered a trifle odd. Some might suggest that the possessor of such thoughts was paranoid, or perhaps that he'd knocked back a few too many Coronas. A few might comment that he was thicker than a hundred-year oak or that he just might be a little too whack-a-doodle for high society. A percentage might even advise their children, wives, and beloved pets to steer clear of the tall man dressed all in black; the one with the aristocratic nose and tiniest of twinkles in his olive green eyes. Some might even be compelled to notify the authorities of a potential lunatic in their midst.

Not so, Gerald Hawkins.

He called the man brother.

Gerald stood at the window of his study, a cup of Earl Grey tea in hand, adoring the yellow-gold rays of morning, and chuckling softly as his twin, Harold, scrutinized the muddy way. Harold bent at the waist, his eyes narrow, his nose fluttering as he inhaled deeply; his senses acutely attuned for the odious odor of renegade substances. Harold paced the ground surrounding the puddle, and then knelt, drawing close to the patch. He would certainly evaluate the composition of the mud. It was not a sloppy, clay-like mud, but more of the watery variety. Gerald knew his brother would recall that it hadn't rained for six days. Nor would he overlook the fact that the remainder of the lawn was as parched as an over-done Thanksgiving biscuit. In some small manner, he hoped that Harold would take samples, pull a kit from his breast pocket, perhaps even evaluate the substance at a molecular level. But this was a bit much to ask, he supposed. The mud, after all, was nothing more than a simple diversion. In retrospect, a handful of dead flies floating in the puddle would have been an amusing touch.

Gerald savored his tea. It was just as he liked it, warm, creamy, safe. Dotty, his housekeeper for some eleven years now, used a specially-sealed tea bag endued with a dye that would release in the presence of toxins. Ah, the tea was wonderful, not a dash of malignancy. Though this did rather take the fun out of it all. Father always got such a kick out of identifying contaminants, extracting the toxins, putting them to good use. Gerald did miss him so. Sometimes he almost wished Harold hadn't been so loyal to tradition. But that would have been poor form. The opportunity had, after all, presented itself. Father would have been furious if Harold hadn't seized the moment.

Gerald focused once again on his brother. Harold had now moved beyond the puddle and was examining a glowing yellow bulb Gerald had placed in the crook of a nearby Maple.

"Dotty," called Gerald. "My brother should make the doorway in no more than ten minutes. How go the preparations?"

Dotty appeared at the top of the winding stairwell. The woman did not look like a "Dotty," thought Gerald. She was much too slender, her curves far too appealing, the breasts too firm, the stomach too flat to belong to a "Dotty." Her hair was long and silky, not done up in some tight and tiny bun. Her eyes were wide and glistening. There was nothing harsh about them, nor was there any hint of befuddlement in her deep blue orbs. No, Dotty should have been a Margaret, or a Heather, perhaps something exotic like Graciela, but not Dotty.

The Dotty who should not have been a Dotty smiled down at Gerald. He could get lost in that smile. "The ventilation has been internalized," she said in a Tara-inspired drawl. "As well, the fruit has been hermetically sealed to prevent tampering."

This woman truly was amazing. "Good, good, very good. Fruits can be quite an issue – especially plums."

Gerald had issues with plums. Severe issues. Run-from-the-house-screaming-like-a-little-girl-confronted-by-a-schoolyard-serial-killer type of issues.

Dotty moved to beside him, nearly close enough to share a stick of gum. Her perfume, some musky blend of intoxicating Middle Eastern aphrodisiacs, made it difficult to concentrate on the task at hand. "I wouldn't worry about compromised plums," she said in a voice that could have belonged to a hospice-care nurse. "That would be poor form."

Gerald pulled away, gazing through the window, attempting to remain focused. "Quite true. You know my brother and his form."

Harold was now making his way up the walkway, scanning this way and that, his keen eyes alert to the slightest deviation from the norm. He had grown up here, after all. He knew what should be where, and where should be what. No rabbit hole was unknown, no shrubbery unaccounted for.

Gerald's throat was suddenly tight. How many years had it been since Harold left the estate? Twelve? No. Thirteen, he supposed. Well over a decade by any account. It had been impractical for the brothers to remain together. Dangerous, unnerving, neither ever knowing the designs of the other. Neither able to sleep soundly. And meals. Meals were nearly impossible. How could one possibly enjoy a casserole? And as to stew! Words could not describe the horror. He gazed at Harold as one might gaze at childhood photographs. Brother. Brother.

A quick sigh, a clenched jaw, and a straightened back, Gerald turned quickly from the window. It was nearly time. "Dotty, would you ask Sarah to play something on the piano? Something lively. I do get so bound up while planning an event."

*****

Harold knocked on the door. Three crisp taps. Never did he ring the doorbell, not once since Auntie Paula's undoing. *Tap, tap, tap.* That was it. No more. No less. Gerald could leave him standing in a rain shower for an hour, but Harold would not knock again. Just *tap, tap, tap*, and wait.

"Hello, Harold," said Gerald as he opened the door, a salamander smile on his round pink face. "Did you enjoy my mud?"

Harold offered a gremlin's grin of his own. "It was just mud, wasn't it?"

"Of course it was just mud. What were *you* thinking it might be?"

The brothers stared silently at each other. Though twins, they were of the paternal sort. Harold was taller by some seven inches. And while Gerald's hair had turned a regal silver at the onset of middle age, Harold's was still dark as India ink in a total eclipse. Gerald was round, Harold lean. Gerald

21

was prone to laughter and sentimentalism, Harold pragmatic as a ledger. Gerald wore loud colors such as purple and yellow. Harold wore black. Always. In short, they were so similar as to be nearly the same person.

Gerald had the sudden impulse to hug his brother, and so it seemed, did Harold. Both took a step forward, arms held wide as if to embrace, and then, simultaneously, they pulled back.

"Ah," said Gerald.

"Agreed," nodded Harold.

A moment of awkward silence, and then, "Who is that playing the piano?"

"Oh," beamed Gerald. "The maid's daughter, Sarah. I find the music soothing."

"I suppose it is, but I do wonder why you allow your help to give her children the run of the house."

"It's called being civil, Harold. I'd think you'd be acquainted with the concept."

Harold stared at Gerald.

Gerald stared at Harold.

"Well, er, come in, come in. You seem a bit pale today. I do hope you're still taking your B complex. You must maintain a healthy liver."

Harold stepped across the threshold, entering his former domicile for the first time in nearly six years. Much too long between visits. He glanced left and then right. His eyes traced the winding staircase to its uppermost step. "Hmmm, yes, well, I'm feeling better than you might suspect. Would you care for a plum? I just picked them this morning." Harold withdrew the small deeply purple fruit from his right jacket pocket, extending it toward Gerald.

Gerald chuckled, shaking his head and willing the blood not to flee his rosy cheeks. It was good to see his brother again. "Harold, not a plum again. Really."

"Gerald, you know better than that. I promised father that I'd never again try to kill you with a plum."

"Yes, but then you killed father with a petrified pomegranate."

Harold shrugged. A fact was a fact.

Gerald led Harold into the dining area and offered him a seat at the dark mahogany table. Harold moved toward the northernmost seat, but Gerald quickly redirected him to the opposing side. Both brothers needed to be in the predetermined place. No surprises – well, as few as possible at least. A plan was a plan, and one must adhere to the plan. That, Gerald knew, was truly good form.

"This one here?" asked Harold with a knowing grin.

"That one will be fine."

"Yes, I did kill father," said Harold as he situated himself at the end of the small rectangular table Gerald had brought out of the basement for just this occasion. "But regardless, I had promised him that I wouldn't try to kill you with a poisoned plum."

Gerald was now seated across from his brother. Even seated, the height difference between the two was glaringly obvious. "True, but don't you see? Since you killed father, that does rather nullify any promises you made him, don't you think?"

Harold seemed to ponder this. His thin upper lip curled ever so slightly as he seemed to gaze off into the nothingness to the right of Gerald's left shoulder. "I suppose it does," he said, finally. "But, still, trying to kill you with a plum again would be poor form."

Gerald offered a curious grin and then shrugged. "Yes, I suppose so. Would you care for some tea?"

"No, no, Gerald. I'm fine as I am." Harold had an unsettled look about his gaunt face. It seemed the eyes settled just a bit deeper in the sockets, the brows drew ever so slightly together, the lips became thinner than single-ply tissue. Harold squared himself in his seat, his posture perfect, his shoulders drawn back with military efficiency. "Do you truly believe me to be so unsophisticated as to attempt the same method twice?"

Ah, so that was it. Harold was offended at the insinuation. Despite his stern demeanor, at the core, the man had always been as sensitive as a feather in the breeze. "No, Harold. I suppose not. No one is more concerned about proper form than my dear, loving brother."

Harold leaned forward. "It was you," he pressed. "That attempted to strangle mother with a garden hose on two separate occasions."

Gerald allowed a tight smile and a silent sigh. "Yes, but I was only ten years-old at the time. Barely old enough to understand the family legacy."

A shrug. "Granted. Yes. But poor form, still."

"I suppose. Yet, it was hardly a garden hose that got her in the end."

"Hardly," agreed Harold. It seemed the color might be returning to his face, though this could be an ominous thing and Gerald tightened as Harold drew breath to speak. "Would you care to recount the tale?"

"Harold, you've heard this telling a dozen times."

A cock of the head, a too-warm grin. "Good form is good form, dear brother. And good form is always better in the retelling." And then a pause. "Now, how about that plum?"

Gerald narrowed his eyes as he leaned forward on his elbows. He had not so much as held a plum in the past eight years. Even at the market, he avoided these devious purple devils as he made his way carefully through the produce department, eyes darting one direction and then the next. He didn't truly believe that some attempt might be made in a place of public presence, but his entire life's existence had taught him to be as cautious as a turtle sans the shell. Slowly, he extended a hand while simultaneously forcing a grin and steadying a hand that so wanted to quiver. "Of course, I'll take your plum, Harold."

The taller man's smile now stretched nearly to his earlobes. "Very well, Gerald. Now, about our dear mother…"

Gerald held the plum in his quivering hand, rubbed his thumb across the cool purple skin detecting no foreign substance. Harold leaned forward, almost imperceptibly, as if in anticipation. "Good form?" asked Gerald.

"Good form," agreed Harold.

Gerald bit into the plum, his teeth penetrating the flesh, his lips pressed against the subtle contour in a kiss fueled by delight and desperation. Juice dribbled down his chin, a drop landing on his upper thigh. Delicious.

"Now, about mother," prompted Harold.

Gerald chanced another bite. The fruit was simply too good. "Yes, about mother. You may remember that you and I were home on break from college and you had just drowned the family dog."

Harold leaned back in his chair, hands folded lazily over his taut belly. He allowed a subtle chuckle. "Of course. Manson. Nice dog."

"Yes. Well, mother and I decided to take a ride down to Kingston's farm. You remember Kingston? He had that kennel."

Another chuckle. A knowing glint. "How could I forget? He tried to sue us after... Mother."

Gerald readjusted in his seat, crossed his legs, and settled in for the telling. "Well, mother and I drove down to Kingston's place. And once we got there...

*****

The air stank of moist hay, wet dogs, and manure. Kingston's place was on the outskirts of town, the more rural – and as far as Gerald's family was concerned, backward – part of town. Though, Gerald felt his clan a bit stuffier than a cream filled donut, mother still considered them all to be above "the menial folk." These, she confided, were considered deficient or incomplete at some genetic level. The Hawkins estate sat atop a grand rise overlooking the entire community. It was, felt she, a palace for royalty, a place from which to gaze down upon the common serfs. Still, even surfs had their place. And despite her rather aloof feelings, she sometimes expressed a certain compassion for these unenlightened "little people." Gerald, for his part, felt the whole thing a bit much. But family was family, after all, and one must play his part. Even to the death, as so often was the case.

Mother Hawkins wore a taffeta dress with a fine mink shawl. Her three inch high heels sank repeatedly into the damp muddy ground as the pair made their way toward the kennels. Gerald held her arm at the elbow, assuring her at least minimal stability on the uneven earth. She was charming he thought. Intelligent. Witty. She would be so proud of him today. He truly

25

hoped she'd live just long enough to appreciate the complexity of his scheme.

"Well, hello, folks. What brings you two down from the top of the hill?" It was Kingston, an average man of average height, average girth, and at least the wisp of a shot at average intelligence.

"We're looking for a new dog," said Gerald with a practiced smile as they strode to within handshake distance of the commoner. A quick glare from mother assured that Gerald did not extend his hand.

"Yes," added mother. "There was an... incident with our previous beast."

"He drowned," added Gerald. "They bloat, you know."

Kingston scratched the back of his head, grunted as only an uneducated man could grunt, and said, "Well, I got thirty 'er forty up ta sell. Pups on up ta three year-olds. What kind you lookin' for?"

Mother stepped forward, a sweet smile on her thinning lips. "Maybe a miniature schnauzer or a sheltie. Something small and cuddly."

Gerald's ears became red. They always became red as he angered. Hadn't they already discussed this? Didn't mother understand? "Large dog!" blurted Gerald, in a manner displaying slightly less sophistication than would an orangutan on Red Bull. "Definitely a large dog."

Mother looked at him, a glint of sadness and pride in her autumn leaf eyes. "Gerald, dear, really. I thought we'd discussed this. You know I want a smaller dog. I'm alone now, with you and your brother off to college, and since Harold dispatched with your father – *before his 401k was vested*, she added silently – it would just be simpler to have a pet I could hold."

What was she doing? This could ruin the entire plan. All of those weeks in plotting. The time spent in research, the money invested to procure just the right equipment. "That's the whole point, mother. You are alone now. You'll need a larger dog to protect you."

"But..."

Her eyes were calling to him now, whispering a silent plea. Gerald couldn't face her. Not now. Not so close. He turned facing the kennels even as he addressed his mother. "At least take a look at them. See if there's any you like."

Mother hesitated. And when she spoke, her tone carried on its breath the resigned timbre of the betrayed. "I suppose I'll look. But only to make you happy. It really is a small dog I'd like, though."

Gerald restrained the impulse to expel a deep and satisfying sigh of relief. "Mr. Kingston, show us the large dog pen, please."

Kingston managed a curious expression as he nodded and said, "Alright, Mr. Hawkins. Just this way."

There were perhaps twelve or thirteen dogs in the pen: three shepherds, a Doberman, a Great Dane, several mixed breeds, and a rottwieler. Mother Hawkins seemed nervous, timid, and just a tad unsteady as Kingston led them to before the chicken wired enclosure. At one point, Gerald thought she just might make a run for it. But that would have been poor form. And mother would never stoop to such. Gerald beamed with love in that moment. Mother was amazing. Oh, how he would miss her.

"There," he said with a dash of pride and a dollop of sorrow. "You see? Look at that rottwieler. Isn't he cute? And that Doberman, very sleek coat." Could he really do this? Could he really follow this through to its inevitable end? "Oh! And three shepherds. Is that a Pit Bull?"

"They're all very nice, dear, but…"

"Mr. Kingston, can mother go into the pen and pet the animals? Perhaps she'll bond with one of them." Gerald had to maintain momentum. To hesitate now could mean failure. Mother would never forgive him if he showed such weakness.

Mother's skin now seemed something akin to aqua in tone. She knew, of course. She had to know. But she was strong. Gerald loved her so in that moment.

"Sure, sure," nodded Kingston. "You can go in too, Mr. Hawkins, if you'd like to join your mama."

"No need, really. Mother is the one who'll be living with the animal."

"Gerald, I'd really rather not. A small dog would be so much more to my liking."

No, no, no, mother. Do not show weakness. Not now. Not in our moment of glory.

Gerald retained his practiced Hawkins grin, though his belly felt as hard as a turnip. "Oh, mother, just pet a few. See how friendly they are."

Mother leaned close to Gerald, whispering in his ear. "Well, they do seem like sweet animals. But, Gerald, dear, you're not trying to… You know…?"

"Kill you?" responded Gerald in a whispered reply. "Good grief, no. I haven't tried that in nearly a decade. Besides, I won't even be in the pen with you. What could I possibly do to harm my dear, loving mother?"

Mother gazed up at him, a subtle glint to her eyes as she reached out to give him a gentle pat on the cheek. "Oh, Gerald, you do care, don't you?"

"Of course I do."

"You're a good son, Gerald."

What was she doing? What was she thinking? Did she really not truly understand that which he'd set in motion? What did she mean by "a good son?" That he would follow through with this or that perhaps he would not? A typhoon of swirling thoughts and doubts tumbled about his brain. Why must mother always complicate things so?

"Well," injected Kingston. "Do you wanna pet some dogs? I can take you over to the small dog's pen if you like."

Mother allowed a determined glace at Gerald, a moment of connection, perhaps of resolve. "This will be fine, Mr. Kingston. Open the pen, please."

The door opened with a whispered creek. Mother strolled through without another word. Tentatively, she petted the closest animal, a shepherd, and then she ventured a pat for a pit bull. Taking another step, she smiled down at the rottwieler. "Look at you. You're so cute. Gerald, you were right. These animals are…"

It was then that the dogs attacked.

Despite his resolve, Gerald couldn't help but avert his gaze from the grizzly sight, though the sounds would linger for months. But, in the last moment, that very precious final breath, mother offered a final affirmation.

"Good form, Gerald. Good form." And Gerald managed a morsel of a smile. Oh, how he loved his mother.

*****

Harold nodded his approval.

Gerald fiddled with the half eaten plumb residing in his palm. "Mother never did choose a dog that day," he added as either an afterthought or as an attempt at black humor. He wasn't quite sure which.

"Wonderful Just wonderful," beamed Harold. "Again, how did you do it?"

Gerald nibbled at the plumb before responding. How he hated that the thing tasted so wonderful. "Just a couple of simple additions to mother's jewelry. Nothing brilliant, really."

"Mother did love her jewelry."

"Mmm, Certainly. Well, what I did was this. I placed a tiny transmitter in mother's necklace. When I pushed a remote button in my pocket, it emitted an ultra-high frequency that drove the animals into a frenzy."

Harold slapped the table with his palm. "Brilliant! Truly, you must be commended. Now, am I correct? There was another devise as well?"

"Yes. In her bracelet. When mother petted the animals, her bracelet brushed against them and they received a mild electric shock."

"Obviously, this antagonized the animals."

"Obviously."

Harold cocked his head, rubbed his nose, and leaned a cat's breath forward. "How's your plum? You haven't eaten it all."

The plum. Yes, the plum. It was part of Harold's strategy. That bit was obvious from the beginning. But, of course, Gerald had a strategy as well. "Delicious, really," he said. "I've just been too busy talking to finish it just yet. Would you pass me a napkin? It's rather juicy."

Harold narrowed his eyes and then offered a razor's edge grin. Slowly, he pulled the drawer situated just under the lip of the table open and withdrew a tan and red cloth.

"No, no," said Gerald. "A blue one please."

Harold nodded and withdrew a second napkin. "Hmm, rather slick to the touch, isn't it?"

"Really? Seems it must not have been properly laundered. Never mind. I'll just use the one you first offered."

"Are you sure?"

"Oh, absolutely." Gerald received the napkin and dabbed lightly at the corner of his mouth. "Now it's your turn. Tell me about Maggie's demise."

Harold's lips stretched to nearly painful proportions, the grin was so wide. "Ah, sweet little Maggie. Our dear little sister."

"I do wish you'd held off until after I'd done mother. Maggie truly would have appreciated my form."

Harold offered a barely perceptible shrug. "Undoubtedly, she would have. I suppose I was just too hasty in my youth."

"Hmmm, weren't we all? Filling father's shoes is no easy task."

"No. None too easy at all."

"So, how did you do it, Harold? How did you kill our dear little sister?"

Harold resettled his stilt-like form in his seat, crossing his left leg over his right, and drumming the fingers of his right hand on the table. He loved talking of this, but held a soft spot for Maggie. His triumph was also his loss. "Well, Maggie, as you may well remember, had a thing for dolls."

"I remember. She had quite a collection."

"Yes, from all over the world. And that, dear brother, is what got me to thinking. You see, Maggie was about to celebrate her eighteenth birthday, and I wanted to do something quite special for her…"

*****

It was mid-July, the twenty-third precisely. Young Maggie's eighteenth birthday. The family had gathered, not just the immediate family, but cousins, uncles, grandparents as well. It was a joyous occasion. A three layer cake sat in the corner like a bride in waiting, and the clan gathered around the living room sofa as the excitable Maggie unwrapped gift upon elaborate gift.

She'd already received an asp tooth supposedly owned by Cleopatra, Ted Bundy's clown nose, and John Wilkes Booth's left molar. It was a joyous time and nothing, it seemed, could dim the mood.

"Oh, my little darling," said mother. "Eighteen already. It seems only yesterday you were running around in diapers, getting underfoot, knocking grandpa into the electric fence."

"I know, mother," giggle Maggie. "You've told me that story a hundred times."

"Well, you know what your father used to say about birthdays."

And here everyone chimed in. For all knew too well what Forest Hawkins thought on the subject. "Make sure to enjoy every birthday. For all you know, it might be your last."

Everyone laughed and chortled, guffawed and cackled. But, Gerald had the tiniest bit of moisture at the corner of his eye. "Sweet, sweet father." He missed him so.

"Yes," agreed Harold. "One of a kind."

"Who'd have thought a quick thunk from a petrified pomegranate would take him in the end."

Harold grinned, his then boyish grin. "Well, I did, actually."

At this moment, Maggie moved to pick up another of her many gifts. Gerald was anxious; he wanted to be next before someone gave her something even more special. "Mine next, Maggie," he said, indicating a purple box toward the back of the stack. "I think you'll enjoy it."

Maggie stood, gave Gerald a quick peck on the cheek, and drew the box to her. "Thank you, Gerald. I'm sure I will."

And she did. It wasn't every girl who received a video box set of "The World's Greatest Executions – extended cut edition." Certainly, she would have enjoyed hours of viewing pleasure. But, Harold's gift was next, and this, by its very nature, would overshadow all else.

"Oh, Harold," exclaimed the excited teen. "A stuffed Genghis Kahn doll!"

"Direct from Mongolia," added the beaming Harold. "Smell it. It's got an authentic fragrance."

It was then that Maggie's sweet and nearly innocent features began to contort. Subtly at first, but then more dramatically as her throat closed shut like a vice grip. It was only through the barest of squeaks that she managed a near imperceptible, "Good form, Harold. Good form." And Harold knew he had done well by her.

*****

"It was in the fabric of the dye, you see," said Harold as he wetted his lips for the conclusion of the tale. "If you'll recall, Maggie used to get a severe allergic reaction to certain textile products. Well, I had the doll custom made with a blend of rare Peruvian fabrics, then directed it to be dyed with extracts from two separate Mediterranean roots, which, when blended, tend to close the airway if inhaled. The combination proved quite effective."

"Quite."

"I do miss her, though. Maggie."

"Ours is not an emotional family, Harold. Don't allow yourself to become sentimental."

Harold's moistened eyes became suddenly dry. His lips, cradling ever such the slightest quiver became as stone. "Sentimental? No. Simply reminiscing. How's that plum coming?"

Gerald eyed the thing. "Oh, fine. Nearly done. You did poison it, I presume."

"Of course."

"I'm sure that you're aware that I have been taking a rather specialized antidote for several years, now."

A grin. A nod. A twinkle of the eye. "Mmmm, yes. That's why I treated it with a destabilizing agent. It essentially causes the components of the antidote to pull apart, reverting to their most elemental components."

"And thus, nullifying the effect. Good form, brother. I hadn't anticipated that."

"And the blue napkin you requested of me – poisoned?"

Gerald set the plum aside and grinned a satisfied grin. "A decoy, really. I spread a bit of lard on it, just to give it that greasy texture. This way you'd assume you'd beaten my attempt."

Gerald caught the faintest glimpse of unease scurry across his brother's features.

"Clever," said Harold. "So, how were you planning on doing it, really? I mean, since the toxins from the plum are already in your system, and you should be gone within a matter of minutes, I would like to know what you'd had in mind."

True, Gerald could feel the effects now. He'd been undone by his brother as he always knew he would be. Such a clever one that Harold. "Oh, my plan is still in effect," he said. "You might have noticed a slight tingling in your legs and toes. You probably thought your feet were falling asleep as they so often do."

"Yes?" Again, a hint of unease. Harold really didn't take well to surprises.

Gerald leaned forward, steadied himself as the world sloshed before him, and then offered a steady smile. "Tiny electrodes in the seat cushion have been emitting a subtle charge, disrupting your neural pathways, immobilizing you. If you were to try to rise just now, you would find yourself entirely incapable of the task."

Harold's face disguised the shock not at all. "Why, Gerald, you are quite right. I am almost entirely immobilized. Though, I fail to see how this alone will accomplish the task at hand."

"That alone, no. But, when used in conjunction with this. Well, that's quite a different scenario altogether." Gerald rose unsteadily, producing from beneath the table a one foot length of green garden hose.

"That? Whatever could you hope for that to do?"

"Ah, you see," said Gerald as he made his way slowly round the table and toward his now immobilized sibling. "I've coated it with a highly conductive substance. Once I tuck this hose-length into the front of your shirt, and tape it right over your chest, the electric pulse from the cushion will be drawn directly up to your heart, interfere with its natural rhythm, and within ten minutes, produce complete, irreversible, heart failure."

"Good form," said Harold as Gerald set about the task of duct taping the hose to the chest. "Good form indeed. My extremities are entirely numb. Why, I can't even lift my arm to pull away that silly hose." Harold paused, seemed to ponder for a moment. His grin returned, though far less broadly than before. "Using that garden hose," he said. "I assume you meant that to be symbolic."

"It just seemed a way to come full circle." His task now completed, Gerald made his way back to his seat. His legs were quite unsteady and it would be entirely ill-mannered to collapse on a teakwood floor.

"You do understand that we now have a bit of a conundrum," offered Harold as Gerald sipped off the last remaining juice from the plum. He had so missed these things over the years.

"The fact that we, the last of our line, are both dying without heirs?"

"Yes, yes. There will be no one left to carry on the family legacy."

At this, Gerald could no longer suppress his grin. Though he was foiled by his brother, still it was to Gerald that would go the prize. "Ah," he said drawing out the word in an exaggerated *Ahhhh*. "But the legacy will remain intact."

Harold's brow furrowed in a most peculiar way. "And how is that?" he asked.

"Through Dotty."

"Your maid?"

"My maid, yes. But more importantly, my wife."

Harold was obviously incredulous. "You've been married and never told me?"

Gerald set aside the plum, steadied himself with the edge of the table, and leaned toward his immobilized sibling. "I knew that you would want the family legacy to be carried on through your line, and so I decided not to tell you about our marriage."

"Because you knew that I would do away with her at first opportunity."

Gerald shrugged. "As would I under the same circumstances."

34

"Of course, of course. And so those little brats running around here…?"

"My children. Our legacy continued for at least another generation."

Harold offered a smile. Though pained, it seemed of the genuine sort. "Good form. Gerald. Good form."

And all was well as Gerald closed his eyes, allowing his head to lull forward on his chest. Good form indeed. Very good form.

THE RESTORATIVE ROOM

They talk of me. They always talk of me. "What to do with Ralph Shaw?" one will say.

"There's an interesting case," adds another, often with a droll expression or a roll of the eyes.

If Dr. Peter Brower is in the room, he might suggest reducing my medication, allowing me a modicum of freedom. Dr. Brower is not quite so deceived as are his colleagues – or so I'm prone to believe.

Dr. Leonard, though. Dr. Bernard Leonard will caution that I'm unstable. That I should spend more time in the room. Dr. Leonard loves sentencing me to the room.

They put me in the room to help me become sane. I can't say that it's been working. I can't even say with certainty that it's necessary. You see, I'm not entirely convinced that, if I'm not already sane, that sanity would be an improvement. The insane, it seems, have fewer worries, fewer encumbrances. When was the last time you saw a lunatic fretting over his mortgage, or incensed that he'd been passed over for a promotion? Does the maniac curse and stomp because of ketchup on a designer shirt, or lie sleepless because of a ding on a bumper? No, the unbalanced among us are concerned with issues of much more import. They're the ones brave enough to speak out against whispering neighbors or intrusive surveillance. They're the ones who understand the danger of *the others*. It seems another word for insanity might be enlightenment. That maybe it's the insane among us who see things most clearly, that it's the muddled mind that sees past the mounting deceptions.

The room, they say, is to be my friend. How can four walls, a floor, and a ceiling be a friend? Can't only a living person, or, at the very least, a living creature of any kind, become a friend, a companion, a confidant? It seems that, perhaps, I'm not the only one suffering from delusions here, that maybe the staff have imagined more for this admittedly complex apparatus, than perhaps it can achieve. But who am I to question? I'm only an inmate, or, as they like to call me, a resident.

The room, though, is quite remarkable. I'll gladly grant them that. Four walls, a ceiling, and a floor, yes, but not entirely. The room is special. As I sit here, on the floor, perhaps ten or so feet from the center, I don't see walls, but rather gaze upon a peaceful forested scene. I see nothing above my head except blue skies with only a hint of cumulous. As I lean back on my palms I feel grass, cool to the touch, just a hint of moisture still clinging from the morning dew. There are no visible walls or fixtures. The scene is seemingly illuminated by the blazing sun; perhaps a bit too hot, but… Maybe I should ask them to turn the sun down a notch.

This place is called the restorative room. Certainly, the name implies that something is to be restored. I'm assuming that, in this instance, the intended restoration is my sanity. Though, peaceful and sedate, I'm still unsure how this setting is meant to accomplish the task. And the expense! Surely the cost of creating a holographic facility such as this must have been astronomical. Wouldn't a simple park have had the same effect? I'm aware of several in the city. They are, for the most part, free, I believe. And some even have concessions.

But, maybe those are all gone now. Maybe the others have poisoned them, ripping the grass from the lawns, blade by blade, replacing it with some vile red filth or oily surface. Maybe this room is all that's left of the reality I've known. Maybe everyone I've ever met or loved is dead. Perhaps, I've been in here for years, decades even, rather than mere weeks. Maybe nothing is as it seems. Maybe nothing ever was.

Or maybe this is just another room, like any other room, and I'm as insane as they claim me to be.

Shhhhh. A deer, do you see it? Standing just beyond the eucalyptus. I'm quite certain it's been monitoring me, maybe recording my movements, my expressions, perhaps even my heart rate. This sounds crazy, I know. But, please remember where I am – a holographic room in a mental facility. Phony animals could, quite easily, be monitoring equipment in disguise. I'll take a look.

Ah, it ran away.

Of course, it ran away.

The facilities keepers wouldn't want me to get too close of a look, now would they? Still, this is interesting. I'd have thought the wall would be closer than it is. And the tree before me, an oak, is so tall, reaching well above where the ceiling should begin. It's coarse to the touch, heavily ridged. Impressive, this illusion they've prepared to help bring the insane back to reality.

There are footsteps now, from behind. Casual, steady. Quite familiar. "Good morning, Ralph," says Dr. Brower as he strolls confidently toward me, clipboard in hand, smile glued to his round and slightly haggard features.

"Where are you really?" I ask. You see, I am not so easily deceived as you might think.

"What do you mean, Ralph?" Still, the Brower thing wears a smile. Always a smile.

"Your anatomy," I say. "You seem well proportioned. Your eyes and hair colors are correct. You've got your notepad as usual."

Brower chuckles. Brower always chuckles. "Well, that's good to know, Ralph."

I step closer, even sneak a quick sniff. Is that cologne I smell? "Not quite so sensible a move is it?" I ask.

"What's that, Ralph?"

"Why risk sending a live person in alone to interview a potentially dangerous psychopath? Wouldn't it make more sense to simply utilize a holographic image?"

"I'm right in front of you, Ralph. You can touch me if you like. Verify that I'm real."

Oh, he would like that, wouldn't he? I could touch him. Maybe on his extended hand as he suspects; or perhaps on the head.

Or on the neck.

Maybe I could snap it like a twig and prove to him that I'm the lunatic he supposes me to be. Or perhaps he'd evaporate from my grasp, and I'd know him to be the holographic lie that I suspect.

"Go ahead, Ralph. Touch my hand," it says.

"I touched the trees, Doctor. They feel real. I touch the grass, it's moist and slick. Though, none of it is genuine."

Again a grin. "Why do you think you've been brought here, Ralph?"

I know what he wants me to say. He wants me to say that I've been brought here to be restored, to become whole again, so that I can return to society, to once again become a productive member. I can recite their goals, their mission for me. Believing it becomes the true difficulty. More likely, I'm here as a guinea pig, a lab rat. The others want to study my reactions to certain stimuli, to determine how best to manipulate the human race.

"Ralph, I asked you a question. Why do you believe you've been brought here?"

I pace to my left, circling him, eying him closely. Certainly, I would not want anyone to presume me predictable. "Why, to be restored," I say." Why else would I have been brought here?"

"That's a very good question," smiles the perhaps/perhaps-not Brower. "Why else would you have been brought here?"

The doctor's clever. Or, at least, the hologram of the doctor is clever. He's trying to determine if I suspect his real motive. He wants to know if I've determined that he's working for the others.

"Why else would we have brought you here?" presses the thing named Brower.

"Oh, Doctor, I don't know. Perhaps you have sensors monitoring my heart rate, maybe even scanning my brain activity. You'll want to learn what aggravates me and what placates me."

A very Brower-like chuckle. "Does that really seem plausible to you, Ralph? Does that seem like something a well-balanced person would think?"

I offer my own chuckle and raise him a guffaw. "Are you telling me, Doctor, that in all the time since I've entered your facility, that you've never monitored my heart, or scanned my brain?"

And now a sigh. No grin. No chuckle. There is always a time when the smile flees the scene of the crime. "Of course we have, Ralph. We've done

CAT scans and MRIs, numerous other tests. You've known about all of these. Our goal is your mental wellness."

Mental wellness or mental servitude? He seems so smug, the doctor. He thinks that with just a few soothing words and a daily dose of medication he can close my eyes to what the outside world has become; that he can distract me from the reality that all is not as it was, that perhaps – most likely, even – it never will be again.

And now the thing we shall call Brower attempts direct eye contact. Oh, it's good. It's very good, very realistic. I could almost believe the lie. Just almost. "Ralph, I believe in being direct with my patients," it says, boring into my soul with that intense gaze. "And so I'm going to be forthright. I'm concerned for you. For some time it seemed we were making significant progress – hence our willingness to allow you times when you're unattended – but now it seems you've relapsed into a state of growing paranoia."

"What's that they say, Doctor? Just because you're paranoid, doesn't mean they're not out to get you."

Another sigh. This one of the exasperated variety. "I'm serious, Ralph. I need you to tell me what you're thinking. I need you to confide in me so that we can work through this together."

Of course, he wants me to tell him what I'm thinking. Isn't that the one thing they can't control? What we think. Isn't that the one refuge left to us, the human race, our minds? If we relinquish control of our thoughts, our motives, then the others will have won. There'll be no place left for humanity to hide.

"Ralph, you seem far away right now. Please. Tell me what you're thinking."

"I'm thinking the sun's too hot. Could you turn it down some? Perhaps a comfortable seventy-five degrees, with a gentle breeze, and just a hint of moisture on the air."

Now the chuckle returns. It's of the ironic sort, but it's a chuckle none-the-less. "Well, that would be nice if it was that simple. But, I think we're stuck with whatever we get." He pauses, studies his notepad for precisely seven seconds before raising his eyes to meet mine. "Again, Ralph, what is it you're thinking when you have those long pauses? Surely, something's going on in your mind. Something more significant than the weather."

Oh, there is something going through my mind alright. I doubt the good doctor would care for it much. I'm wondering how to escape this room. I'm wondering how realistic this holographic doctor really is. If I were to wrap my fingers around his neck and squeeze, would he continue with the illusion? Would he allow the holographic doctor to perish, or would he break this false reality and show me the true nature of this room, the true nature of himself, and this twisted world he and the others have created?

I wonder.

"Ralph, you're doing it again. What were you thinking just then?" There's worry on his face. Genuine concern. How entertaining.

"Doctor Brower, are you really sure you want to know *all* that I've been thinking?"

"As much as is possible, Ralph, yes. I believe in therapy over medication. I want to help you discover the root of your illness, to help you deal with the underlying issues. I can only do that if we're both entirely open with one another."

"Hmmm, being open. Is that what this is all about?" I step toward him now, quickly, leaning as if to angle one direction and then switching to the other. "Well, let me explain what I'm thinking – doctor. You see, I don't believe that you're being open with me. In fact, I don't even believe that you're real. Not that you're really here, at least. Oh, you might be in the next room, observing, speaking through this holographic monstrosity before me. But, this isn't you in front of me."

I'm upon him now. Quickly, I can move so quickly when properly motivated. The flesh feels as real as did the tree bark. I can feel the pulse racing, the sweat moistening the skin, the airway collapsing. It's almost as if I'm strangling a real live human being. How very curious.

The doctor seems so lifelike as I lower the holographic corpse to the ground, grab hold of each ankle, and begin dragging it toward the nearby holographic stream. Truly, I thought he'd break the illusion. That he'd allow me to see this facade for what it truly is, a hoax, a myth. But then, why would he do that? Better, he allow me to question myself, to ponder, to wonder if, just perhaps, I've been wrong all along, that maybe I have just killed the real Dr. Peter Brower.

That would be sad, traumatic even. I respect the doctor. True, I believe he works for the others, that he's their stooge, their informant, but I don't really think the doctor entirely realizes with whom he's aligned.

There I go again. Thinking of him as if he's still alive, when I know in my heart that he's...

No. He is alive.

Dr. Brower is most definitely still alive. I'm in the restorative room. Everything here is holographic. It's unreal. There's nothing of substance here. Not the animals, not the people. Certainly not the man I've just killed.

So heavy, though, dragging this holographic body toward the rippling water. Strange, I feel the need to dispose of it, to hide my imagined crime. Nothing criminal has happened. The man was an illusion. In all truth, why would the real Dr. Brower come in here? He knew my history, knew my potential to break with reality, knew my propensity for violence.

There I go again. Thinking of him in the past tense. As if I'd truly squeezed the life out of him. As if that stream I'd just thrown his body into was truly water running from one point to another.

The stream.

The body.

Yes, the body was truly heavy. I'm still winded. In fact, my muscles even ache.

Perhaps...

Perhaps a test. Yes, a test. Step into the "stream," see how real the sensation can become, how true a false image can seem.

Yes, a test. Simple yet effective.

Wet.

I feel quite wet. How interesting. And taste. It tastes cold. Slimy. Full of sand. No. No, this is just too real. The illusion too perfect.

Ah! Wait. Yes. Yes, I see it now. Where they tripped up, where they inched just a bit too far into the realm of the real. How could anything associated with this place be that perfect, that tangible, unless it was false? Oh, they almost got me. They truly did. They had me thinking that just maybe I had really killed Dr. Brower. But, that just doesn't make sense. This is a mental facility. I'm a mental patient. I'm on medications. Why would the doctor, knowing how volatile I am, come out here alone? No matter how much he talked of transparency and openness, would he really risk his own life in order to prove his trust in me?

And this place. This room. What am I to believe of it? That it's truly as it seems? A quaint, peaceful park adjacent a mental ward? No. That makes no sense. It'd be too easy for me to flee, to make my way into town, to never come back. Even with the barbed fence in the distance, surely there would be a means of escape. Of course I'm really in a room. Of course all that I see is an illusion. It's the only logical explanation.

"Is that really what you believe, Ralph?"

"Dr. Brower?"

"Do you really believe that this is all a holographic illusion? Or are you just telling yourself that because you can't bear to face the truth of your life?"

"But, you're dead."

"I was under the impression that you thought none of that was real."

"Yes, well, of course it's not, but…"

"But, what, Ralph?"

"But, still, I thought… Nothing."

"Are you sure about that, Ralph? Are you sure it was nothing? Are you sure that's not really my flesh beneath your fingernails, that it's not really my body floating down that stream? Are you sure of that, Ralph?"

He's pushing me. Goading me. Trying to get me to reveal what I really know about the others. About him and this room.

"Is that true, Ralph? Am I goading you? Who are these "others" you keep thinking about?"

How does he do that? Dr. Brower was never able to hear my thoughts before. Do they have some new technology, alien perhaps?

"No technology, Ralph, alien or otherwise. Is that who you think the others are – aliens? Is that what you think this is all about?"

He's doing it again. Reading my thoughts.

"Reading your thoughts? Perhaps that's what you would call it. Though, there are other explanations as well."

"Stop it! Why are you doing this to me?"

"Oh, I don't know, Ralph. You did, after all, just kill me. That can cause a guy to be cranky."

"I did not! I didn't kill you! You were just a hologram, a fake!"

"Really? I sure seemed real to me."

He's trying to confuse me. It's the others. He's working for the others, as some sort of spy that can read my thoughts. He's their agent. He has been all along. There never was a real Peter Brower.

"Ralph, I'm right here. Please talk to me instead of about me."

"You're not here! Not this time! Not…"

"Not what, Ralph?"

"Not like before."

"I'm not sure I know what you mean, 'not like before.'"

He's clever. Oh, this one is clever. Far more so than the other Dr. Brower. The one I…

Never mind.

This one seeks to trick me, to confound me using my own thoughts. It's almost as if he's using my mind against me. But, he doesn't fool me. Not anymore. Oh, he had me for a moment. Had me doubting my very senses, doubting what I know to be true. But, once again, Dr. Brower is not what he seems. He's not the real doctor. The real Dr. Brower would never goad me such. And he's not a figment of my mind either. For, how could my own thoughts be so antagonistic toward my well-being?

No. the answer is simple. Obvious. This is another hologram. I killed one false doctor, and now the others want to see if I have the fortitude to kill another. That's it of course. I'm in the restorative room. A holographic mechanism within a mental facility. Nothing that has happened in here is real. Not any of it. I am whole. I've killed no one today.

No one!

Hmm, I wonder where he's gone off to. He was here. Right here, standing before me, that cheeky grin on his smug and troubling face. But, now…

But, now…

I think it best that I sit down. That's it. Just sit. Sit and relax. Breathe. Sit. The sun moves to the supposed west.

Still, I sit.

The shadows lengthen, the temperature drops ever so slightly.

I sit.

I wonder…

I wonder when Dr. Brower's going to come by. It seems he should have visited by now. But, maybe… It's the room. The restorative room. It's designed with alpha waves, vibrations that muddle the mind, that make it hard to concentrate, to think clearly. I need to think. There's something important. I need to… I need to… I wonder if they can turn the sun down some. It's so bright in here. The others like it bright. They always like it bright.

This room, it is amazing, isn't it? The sun, the breeze. Maybe it truly does restore. Though, the creek is a bit unsettling. I could do without the creek.

Strange, I used to like the babbling water, with its peaceful gurgle and lilting splash. But now it's disquieting. I suppose I should ignore it. That's the solution. Turn away from the creek. Ignore.

A sound.

Do you hear it?

The likeness of a door opening and then closing. Yes, and then footsteps. Slow even footsteps approaching on grassy ground. How serene.

Ah! Ah-ha. The nurse. Julie is her name, or so I've been led to believe. "Hello, Nurse Julie," I say, ever the social butterfly that I am.

"Ralph, still sitting on that bench? I'd have thought you'd be up walking around, enjoying the beautiful scenery." She smiles a practiced nurse smile. They all have the same smile, these nurses. All of them.

"No, nurse. I seem to be a little worn today."

"Well, how about a nice meal? Yankee pot roast tonight. Your favorite."

She touches me on the shoulder, a simple kindly gesture. She seems real enough. I had, after all, heard the door open and then close. I'd heard her approach from the distance. This is no proof of her reality – of course not – these things can be so easily replicated. Still, there is a certain level of trust. Or, if not trust, openness at least.

"Nurse?"

"Yes, Ralph."

"Dr. Brower, did he come by today?"

She smiles the practiced nurse smile, cocks her head in the practiced nurse way. "Of course he did, Ralph. You know he always checks in on you. Though, I do seem to have lost track of him. You know how he is, this way and that. But anyway, he left instructions with me to take you to the others. I'm sure you'll find them very interesting."

"The others?"

"Yes, Ralph. They're waiting for you in the TV room."

I angle my head in her direction, apparently offering a quizzical expression. I'm prone to these, I know, and have been told they can be somewhat unnerving.

"What is it, Ralph? You have a peculiar look on your face."

"Oh, I was just wondering, nurse, just exactly how real you are. Though, I suppose we'll just have to find out, won't we?"

LIBERTY'S FALL

It is said that whatever a man is when in the living, even more so he will be beyond the grave. That for those troubled souls who, for whatever reason, have not yet moved on to their final destination, for those who linger but a cat's breath from this tortured physical plain, that these are destined to increase in their excesses to a point of manic extreme and often irreversible insanity.

*****

The green luminescent numbers of the clock stared uncaringly at Liberty Marks in mocking silence. 2:32 AM. Another sleepless night. How many had this been now? Five? Six? No, seven. An entire week with perhaps ten hours sleep cumulative. This couldn't continue indefinitely, she knew. But, for the moment, it was what it was. Her mind was already in gear. Sleep would not come.

It was probably the Hoffman account that stole her slumber. That damn Hoffman account. How could that have gone to Horace McKenzie? Liberty had earned that account, had fought hard for it. It had been her efforts more than any other's that had sealed the deal. What difference did it make that McKenzie was a more senior salesperson? Yes, Horace did contribute to the deal. No one could dispute that. But it was Liberty who set the foundation. It was Liberty who initiated contact. Liberty who whittled out the details, working compromises that Horace McKenzie would never dare offer, that regional manager, Chris Farris, would never approve, had he known the minutia of the details.

Chris Farris. There was the problem. Chris was squarely in McKenzie's back pocket. What an oaf. Suck down another donut and kiss McKenzie's patootie, that was Chris Farris.

Liberty glanced at her husband. Seth slept like a grizzly in January, oblivious to her insomnia. Stealthily, she rose, crossed the room and opened the door to the adjacent hallway. Might as well let the day begin. There was still a lot of work to do on the Cronin account, and God knew she didn't want Chris Farris passing that one on to the geezer. She didn't understand why it was such a crime to be in her mid-twenties, to be driven, to be capable. Why was it that no one took her seriously? Was it such a horrible thing to be young, attractive, upwardly mobile? Apparently some thought so. Well, screw them. Liberty could blaze her own path. The unmotivated, the complacent, they might be able to slow her now and again, but in the end, her sheer verve would overcome such minor nuisances. Liberty would overcome. She would excel. That was simply who she was. A winner.

*****

Seven more days now. Liberty had managed two solid night's sleep and a couple of five hour near misses. She felt better, more alert. A bit more focused. She knew she'd need to back off on the energy drinks, though. They made her jittery while, each day, becoming less effective. Liberty left Chris Farris's office with an odd feeling in her gut. It had been ten days since she'd come to her manager concerning Horace McKenzie's self-medication issues. She'd almost felt bad about snitching on the old coot – almost! – But it was something the boss should know. Or so she told herself. Now, she only hoped Farris would actually address the issue. He and McKenzie were close. She hoped Farris wouldn't sweep this under the rug. If so, she might need to go over even his head. Still, it had been a few days since she'd seen McKenzie at his desk. Maybe Farris had been man enough to tackle the issue after all. Either way, it was probably better if Liberty didn't broach the subject again. Best not to appear too anxious. Let McKenzie and Farris dig their own holes. Then maybe Liberty could sideline them both in one easy move.

She paused. There was something else troubling her about McKenzie. Something significant concerning him, about why he'd been away, perhaps, or maybe even...

Huh.

Why was it she couldn't grab hold of that thought? She knew it was important, knew she should know this detail. She shook her head, chuckled at her mild confusion. No matter. It would come to her.

Making her way through the office, Liberty smiled at Don Haler, a new account exec. She was certain he had a thing for her, and even encouraged his little crush with whispers and winks, with subtle – nearly accidental – physical contact and a well-selected wardrobe. Don was cute in a frat boy kind of way, and besides, it never hurt to have someone in her corner when interoffice issues arose. If the kid thought he might get some, he'd land squarely on her side no matter his true feelings on the topic at hand. Liberty could not understand why so many attractive women felt so cursed by their beauty. Didn't they understand the tool they'd been given? And if once and a while a girl had to put out to get what she wanted, what was the harm? The rest of them would do the same if they had the opportunity.

Liberty strolled into her cubicle and slid into the seat, hoping to work on the Dugan file while inhaling a tuna sandwich, all before her one o'clock meeting with McCarthy and Birch. She set her laptop computer on the desk and withdrew the sandwich from her purse as the Compaq fired up.

"Well, who have we here? Liberty Marks."

"McKenzie?" Great. How had she missed him standing there? The last thing she wanted was the coot staring over her shoulder as she pounded out the details for a new client.

But again, there was something else. Something about McKenzie that churned her stomach, that caused her flesh to creep just a little, that made the blood slow in her veins and her gut to tighten like a Super-Ball. She couldn't quite place it. Something she'd heard about the man, perhaps? Maybe it was just some misguided guilt about turning the old guy in to Chris on that little substance issue. Whatever the case, she wasn't going to be productive if Horace remained.

"What seems to be the problem, Liberty? It looks like you may have had a bit of a day already."

Liberty forced her cover girl smile. "Not a thing, Horace. Just not quite enough sleep these days."

"Oh, too much on your mind?" asked the tall thin man as he draped his navy blue jacket over a chair and turned to face Liberty. Somehow he seemed more vibrant, perhaps a bit more substantial than he had – what? A week ago – the last time they'd talked. "Well, don't worry your pretty head too much," added McKenzie. "You don't even know what real trouble is yet."

It took a moment for the statement to set in, and then Liberty nearly screamed. Chris Farris had no spine. No spine at all. Obviously, he'd told McKenzie that it was Liberty who'd come to him about his drinking on the job.

"Horace, listen. I don't know what Chris Farris has said to you, but…"

"I'm not at all concerned with Chris Farris," shot McKenzie in a near hiss. "Isn't there something else that concerns you more than your petty little power schemes?" There was condensation in the voice. Resentment.

Something about McKenzie was nettling at her. Something she was forgetting. Something she'd been told. Damn, she wished she'd slept better. Her mind was never this fuzzy.

"You really put your foot in it, didn't you?" McKenzie's voice was firm yet smooth. A coaxing voice. A salesman's tone.

"What are you talking about?"

"Getting married, raising a family, all when your inner ambition is success, to rise to the top of your field. You are very driven, Liberty. Seth is holding you back. Your daughter Carly as well."

"Horace, I resent that. You have no idea what you're talking about."

"Oh, yes," chortled the coot. "Seth is unmotivated, inferior. And Carly? Yes, of course she is wonderful, hmm? But tell me the truth; you're not yet willing to give up your freedom just to mother some snot-nosed brat through diapers and beyond. If only you hadn't gotten pregnant in college. If only you hadn't allowed Seth to 'do the right thing,' and marry you. Liberty, you would be so much further in her career."

"That's a load of crap."

McKenzie chuckled as he drew closer to her, his slate blue eyes locked with Liberty's own. His too-narrow fingers came together, intertwining, working as if at some unseen puzzle. "Oh, silly, naïve Liberty. At least be honest with yourself. You want my job. You have for some time." Another step closer. A tilt of the head. A glint of perfect white teeth. How could a man his age still have perfect teeth? "And the job is yours," he added with a leer. "It's waiting for you as we speak. You should know this already. Really, I think you do. You've just temporarily forgotten a thing or two."

What was the coot getting at? Surely he had some game here, some angle. And why was she so unnerved. McKenzie was on the way out. She'd made sure of that. Something was wrong. Something was very wrong.

And still, deep down she was certain that she knew what it was, that the truth was like a feather on the breeze, floating just beyond her grasp. Why was the truth so elusive, so cagey?

"Liberty. Dear Liberty. You seem a touch pale. You are feeling well, I hope."

"Listen, Horace, things are fine. You're fine – just nosey, I guess. And mildly obnoxious. I don't know what you're talking about, but you can keep your job."

"Oh, I can? A bit late for that, hmmm?" Horace stepped closer. His grin was horrible, his skin too smooth, his hair too dark. Why did he seem a man thirty years his own junior? "You come in here, all driven, trying to prove yourself, working extra hours, showing everyone up. You insert yourself into my negotiations – with my clients. I lost my wife over my clients, Liberty. They are my family. But, you… Why, you could push a man to have a stroke."

Hands quivering, Liberty closed her laptop without bothering to turn it off. What was happening to her? She was exceptional. She was one to thrive. How was it this geezer – this admittedly young and handsome geezer – had come to unnerve her so? "Horace," she said in an effort to regain control of the conversation. "You're being rude. I work hard. So what?"

"Hmmm, and all the while, Miss Perfect hides something from her husband. Something significant."

Liberty's stomach dropped five stories. "Horace, what are you talking about?"

A smile. An oh so broad smile. The grin of an executioner with his hand on the gallows. "A certain test result that might, shall we say, change some things."

"My God, how could you know about that?"

"Some things are obvious, Liberty, if one only cares to look."

And those titanium eyes locked on her, and grew, and grew, and grew, until all there was in the world were those two subzero orbs.

*****

"Morning, Libby," said Seth as Liberty shuffled into the kitchen after yet another near-sleepless night. "I hope sunny side up is fine. Carly already ate. She's upstairs brushing her teeth."

Liberty grunted through an exasperated sigh. She hated that Seth tried to care for her. Sure, he meant well. He was concerned with being a good husband and father. But, why? Truly, Liberty could tend to her own needs. He didn't need to romance her or coddle her. Just let her be. And as to Carly, well, she supposed at least Seth dealt with that little setback. She wondered how he'd deal with the next one – especially considering the circumstances. Of course, as far as Liberty was concerned, there was no need Seth ever know those particular circumstances.

Making a stop by the coffee maker, Liberty then nearly fell into her seat at the table. Seth appeared almost immediately beside her with a perky kiss and a plate full of runny eggs. "Seth, why are you doing this?"

"Doing what?"

Liberty allowed another sigh. The guy had no clue. He never had. Of course, what could she expect from a guy who made his living sitting at his computer designing mindless video games for a third rate company on a fifth rate salary? "Fixing breakfast for me, Seth. Waiting on me. Why do you insist on doing it?"

"Um, because I love you."

Idiot!

"Don't you have any ambition of your own? Isn't success important?"

"Uh, honey, they're just eggs."

Liberty shook her head. Why fight it? At some level Seth's temperament allowed her to focus on more important matters than the nonsense at home. "You're right, Seth," she said through a loveless smile. "I'm sorry. Things at work are just a little stressful right now."

She paused, sipped her Folgers, glanced at the murky liquid and nearly dropped the mug to the floor. Had that been a face she'd seen? Not a reflection, not her own distorted features staring back at her, but the face of a man, young, vibrant, a stranger and yet anything but? She looked again. Nothing.

Liberty.

The voice came from behind her.

Liberty.

No. To her right.

What was that wavering form slithering toward Seth?

Liberty shook her head attempting to rid the image. Seth was there. Right there. But there was another image as well, shadowy, indistinct. And then the figure was behind and to the right of Seth. The figure of a man. McKenzie. Grinning. Chuckling. His hands clasped about Seth's neck as if to choke the life from him.

You don't need him, Liberty. Don't need him at all. Baggage. Too much baggage for one such as you.

A quick jerk of Seth's head.

A horrendous snap.

Liberty blinked.

She blinked again.

The image was gone.

Jittering, she set her mug on the table and covered her face with her palms. It was the lack of sleep. It had to be the lack of sleep.

"Libby, you okay, Hon? What's the matter?" Seth was there now, beside her, stroking her hair, attempting to comfort her.

Liberty steeled herself, took a deep breath, held it for ten seconds before releasing it slowly. "Have I ever mentioned Horace McKenzie?" she asked through a labored gasp.

Seth squinted, cocking his intact head on his undamaged neck. "I don't think so. Who is he?"

Liberty slid her palms over her forehead and to the base of her neck. "No one that matters. Just this weird guy at work. Creepy. Nosy."

Seth's normally placid face was tight with concern. The idiot probably thought he needed to protect his wife – as if she was the fragile one! "Has he done something to you?"

A shake of the head. An averted glance. In no known universe could she reveal what she'd just imagined. "No... He's just odd, I guess. There's something about him. Something, I'm not sure. Nothing."

You don't need him, Liberty. Baggage. Too much baggage.

"Lib, you don't look like it's nothing. You look scared to death."

"It's nothing, Seth. Nothing!" snapped Liberty. "Just leave me alone – alright? Just go play Mr. Mom. Everything's fine."

*****

Liberty had trouble concentrating that day and so picked up her laptop and relocated to the break room. New scenery. New attitude. Or so, that was the thought. She sat gnawing on an apple as she fought to piece together a proposal for an orphaned client named Gonzales. One of the newer reps, a kid named Scott Sanders, had left it dormant when he'd abruptly left the company. Liberty knew why he'd left – the truth of why he'd left. She carried his child. Sanders didn't want the responsibility and Liberty didn't want the complication. Better to let Seth believe what he would long to believe. Better for everyone concerned.

"Hello, Liberty."

"Horace? When did you sneak in here?"

"How are things at home? Is Seth well? Are you sleeping at night?"

"Fine. Everything's fine."

"Now, I know better than that."

Liberty was sweating. Why was she sweating? And cold. Suddenly, her skin was covered in goose bumps.

And yet she sweat.

McKenzie straddled a chair across from Liberty. His coal black hair glistened in the neon light and his icy blue eyes accented his knowing grin. "You want your freedom, Liberty. You feel saddled with the responsibility of a growing family right when your career is taking off. You're carrying dead weight."

Liberty tried to pull her gaze free of the man, but he drew her into him: closer, closer. Why had she never noticed how attractive he was? How was it she'd ever thought of him as a coot? Horace McKenzie was outright gorgeous. He rose, smiled sensuously as he made his way to around the table. He was lean, muscular. She could actually see his muscles ripple beneath his crisp white business shirt. And now he was here. Standing above her. Gazing down. She cocked her head, parted her lips. At the last she closed her eyes, just as he leaned in toward her, just as his lips brushed against her own. "Yes," she said in a whisper. "Yes."

And then she was alone.

*****

Liberty had no idea why Chris Farris had called her to his office. The man was weak, ineffective, unmotivated. Too much like Seth to ever be truly successful in his position as regional manager. But, he was the boss, and Liberty had no choice but to come scampering at his beckon. She just hoped he wouldn't drone on about whatever his issue was this time. Probably that she'd given too steep a discount to Henderson Mills. Well, tough. A client that size, the company could absorb the cost. "You wanted to see me?" smiled Liberty as she slid into a faux leather chair and then leaned forward accentuating her cleavage. Whatever the problem, Liberty was a master of distraction.

Farris nodded, grunted, shook his head as if to shake away a distraction. "Um, yes." A pause. Another shake of the head. "You've been producing excellent numbers, Libby. You're outgoing, dynamic."

What a load of bull. What was he driving at?

"Why, thank you Chris. That means a lot to me."

"Well deserved, Libby. Well deserved." Chris took a quick snatch of a Snickers bar and adjusted himself in his seat, attempting to get comfortable. He was a large man and no matter what angle he claimed, still the office chair seemed to enslave his mid-section. Pathetic. How could anyone allow himself to live that way?

"Chris? You had something to say?" The man was gazing off into nowhere. What? Was he on some trippy sugar high or something?

"Oh, uh, Libby, I'd like to have you take over the cliental of one of our senior men."

"Yes?" prodded Liberty. Why was Farris being so air-brained?

"It would certainly mean more hours, a more hectic schedule, and of course, the potential for much larger commissions."

Interesting. She hadn't expected this. Well, not today, at least. She'd earned the position, of course, but hadn't thought Chris Farris bright enough to notice. "Whose position would I be taking? Did someone retire?"

Chris's ample face dropped. He seemed truly surprised by her question. "Oh, Libby. I'm sorry. I thought everyone knew. It's Horace McKenzie's position. He passed last week. A stroke."

*****

The music was a loud, driving, monotonous, *thump, thump, thump*. Club music. The kind that one can only enjoy in a place crowded with half-drunk horny strangers. The kind of place Liberty had abandoned upon becoming a respectable wife and mother. The kind of place she retreated to when the sane world seemed too crazy for her to inhabit.

McKenzie could not be dead. He couldn't be. She'd seen him. Touched him. For God sake, she'd kissed him. Kissed the coot. No. Not the coot. McKenzie, yes. But...

"Hello, Liberty."

"Horace?" There he was. Perfect. Magnificent. Leo DeCaprio, Brad Pitt, George Clooney. Whatever male ideal one could imagine, Horace McKenzie embodied it – eclipsed it even. She was embarrassed by the sudden tingle racing through her form. Somehow, she knew he'd be aware of her blatant need.

"It's me, Liberty. Don't be embarrassed. Your desire is only natural."

She blushed, turned a half profile, stared down at her feet. "Chris said that you were dead."

He was behind her now, gripping her shoulders in his palms, pressing his chest against her back. "Believe what you see, Liberty. Not what you hear."

"But, you're different. Not old. Not…"

"I am as I've always been. Trust me, Liberty. You need to trust me." He paused as his right hand slipped away, only to return in but a second bearing a shot glass. "Would you care for a drink?"

"Um… No thank you, Horace. I'm…"

"Pregnant. Yes. That little whelp Sanders had more potency than I'd imagined. Drink, Liberty. It'll ease your tension."

"But…"

"Drink, please. It's very important that you accept something from me. Very important."

It seemed his voice surrounded her, that it became one with the throbbing, pulsing beat. And those eyes. Those gorgeous eyes. Deep. Cool. Reflective. How could she have ever refused those eyes?

The alcohol burned as it slid down her throat. And there was another drink, near instantaneously. And another. Burning, sealing, establishing. So good. So good.

"Yes, Liberty," cooed McKenzie. "Seal the deal. You and I. We have business to attend to."

*****

Seth was such a square. Why did he make such a deal about her having a few drinks after work? True, she'd had a teeny little accident. True, he'd had to borrow money from his snooty old mother to bail her out of jail. But, Seth had no sense of adventure. No flare. Not like Horace. No, not like Horace at all.

"What were you thinking?" he screamed as they crossed the threshold into their sparsely-furnished living room. He actually had the gall to scream at her.

"A little celebration. I got a promotion. Unlike you, I'm going to make enough money to get us out of this little rat trap and into a respectable home."

"Libby, you had a blood/alcohol level of three times the legal limit. You swerved across three lanes of traffic. You could have been killed."

"Oopsie!"

"Libby, you know your history. This was something we've talked about. This was…"

"I'm my own woman, Seth."

His face was red. He looked like a zit about to pop. "You're my wife! I deserve at least a little consideration!"

He thinks he can control you, Liberty. He thinks he owns you. That you're his property to order about as he pleases.

She wasn't sure where the knife came from, or how it happened to be in her hand. But there it was; Norman Bates approved: gleaming, sharp, deadly. Seth's eyes went wide. "Do you know what you deserve, Seth? Hmm? Do you know?"

She stepped closer. He backed up, jabbering some nonsensical syllables.

"I'll tell you what you deserve."

Tell him, Liberty. Tell him.

The knife was over her head now, poised to strike.

"I'll tell you exactly what you deserve."

She clutched tighter, tighter. Seth was pinned back against the wall now, no place left to flee.

And the knife came down in one swift movement.

And clattered against the ceramic floor.

Useless.

Had she nearly done that? Had she nearly killed her husband? And for what? Because he was angry that she'd nearly been killed while drunk driving? She couldn't even remember the evening. Couldn't have told him how she'd come to be on that road, why she'd drank so much – what it was she'd even consumed.

Somehow she found herself in his arms. For some insane reason he received her. And insane it was, for the knife was still within reach and Liberty was not yet sure she wouldn't use it.

*****

Another day. Another hour. Another sales call. Liberty massaged her forehead, attempting to concentrate on the conversation. "Yes, Mr. Cribbs… Yes, I understand the order was late… No, there is no excuse… I'm sorry, sir. I'm really not sure what happened… You're right, sir. My fault entirely. I…"

And the phone line went dead. He'd hung up on her. He'd actually hung up on her. Another account going south. Liberty closed her eyes, kneaded her temples with her fingertips. She wanted this day to be over. She needed to get some sleep before she bankrupted herself.

There was now a pressure on her shoulders. Strong hands, rubbing, gripping, pressing deep into the tissue, releasing the tension within. "No. Not yet, dear girl. You're on the rise, climbing the ladder. No time for self-pity."

"Horace, I can barely see, I'm so tired. Everyone else has been gone for three hours."

"And that's why we'll be number one. Remember, we're a team, Liberty. You and I to the grave."

Liberty nodded and reached for her mug. Another shot of caffeine. Another gulp of confidence. Horace was right. Of course, he was right. Horace was the master salesman. No one knew better than Horace.

"Now, Liberty, the Mulligan account. The man has needs. We can fulfill those needs. Call now, he'll be there late. I know these things."

Liberty shook her head, attempting to clear her fuzzy vision. These last few weeks, since she'd partnered with Horace, they were a blur. She just didn't know how much longer she could keep the pace. "Horace, I need to go home. Need to sleep. I've got to talk to Seth about the baby. Any day I'll begin to show. I need…"

"The baby?" scoffed Horace. "You don't even want that child. You're career, woman. You drove me to the grave for your career. Now, you'd better make the best of it."

"Horace, I can't concentrate. I'm just too tired. You keep pushing and pushing. My sales are slipping. We're losing accounts. I can't keep this pace."

"George Palmer's desk, second drawer on the right. A green pill bottle. Take two, no three. Take three. Those will get you going. There are cigarettes there too."

"I don't smoke."

"Start. They'll calm you."

"Pills to perk me up, cigarettes to calm me. Isn't that a contradiction?"

Horace was before her now, face to face, his cold steel eyes locked with her own. "It's the road to success, Liberty. It's the choice you've made. Success is all that matters. Isn't that what you used to say? More important than family. More important than integrity, honor. This is you, Liberty. At your core. This is us. Now, hit those phones. There's money to be made."

Hesitantly, Liberty reached for the cool, lifeless receiver. It seemed her entire body was afire, that some strange energy emitted from Horace. Someone was on the phone now. Had she even dialed? "Yes? Um, Mr. Mulligan? Yes, this is Liberty Marks from…"

And Liberty's life tumbled into a kaleidoscopic blur…

July…

August…

September…

October…

"Libby, may I see you in my office?"

"In a minute, Chris. I've…"

"Now, Libby. That call can wait."

Liberty replaced the receiver, and, offering a mock salute, swiveled toward the stern-looking Chris Farris. "Well, sir-yes-sir."

Rising, she followed Farris into his corner office. As usual, the room smelled of pizza and burgers. Pathetic.

"Have a seat, Liberty."

Liberty complied, sitting on the padded seat before the cluttered and slightly blemished desk.

Farris lowered himself into his power seat and leaned forward, elbows on the desktop. His white, short sleeve business shirt was stained yellow at the pits, and the man's orange and blue tie hung cockeyed from his neck. "Libby, you've always been an exemplary employee. You've been very organized, punctual. I wish I could have cloned you."

Despite her boss's dire demeanor, Liberty offered a wry smile. "I think there are laws against that, Chris."

Farris leaned further forward, a halfhearted attempt at creating some sort of bond. "My point is that you are no longer that employee."

What kind of bull was this? "I work harder than anyone here."

A nod, accompanied by an embarrassed shrug. "Yes, you do. You're here late into the evening – yesterday, until two in the morning. Your eyes are always bloodshot, your hair disheveled. Sometimes you're still wearing the same clothes you had on the day before. Libby, you're working yourself to death."

"I'm doing my job!"

Another nod. "You're working hard, yes. But, since taking over Horace McKenzie's file load, you've lost five of his long term accounts. Five, Libby. Do you have any idea how long it took Horace to nurture that business, to bring those clients on board?"

"He sounds like your husband, Liberty. He sounds like your husband who sounds like he's trying to be your father." It was Horace. He'd come up behind her, whispered into her ear – perhaps directly into her brain.

"You sound like my husband, Chris. You sound like my husband who sounds like he's trying to be my father."

Chris nearly dropped his fat jaw to his desk. "Libby, I'm being serious, here."

A mocking impersonation from Horace. "Libby, I'm being serious, here."

And from Liberty. "Libby, I'm being serious, here."

Chris Farris sighed, dropped his head for perhaps five seconds, and then met her gaze. "Okay, listen. I'm not sure what's going on in your home life."

"Liberty, I don't believe the man belongs in your business."

"None of your business, Chris!"

"But, Libby, you can't let your personal life effect your professional life."

"Tell him, you only have one life."

"I only have one life."

Chris passed his palm over his face, closed his eyes for a moment, and then steadied his gaze. "Libby, I can't believe it's come to this, but either you get your life under control or I'm going to have to let you go."

Let go? How could he even consider...? She was his superstar. She was the up-'n-comer. She was... She was what? What was she anymore? Who was she? Somehow, she simply didn't know.

*****

It was nine-thirty in the evening. The office was deserted except for Liberty. She'd just sent off an email to Chris Farris and now sat staring at the unused phone. It beckoned to her like a charmed snake, but she simply stared beyond. It was over. She'd told Seth everything: the baby's true parentage, her growing dependence on stimulants, and as best as she could understand it, Horace. Surely, he'd thought her insane. Who would not? But, Seth was of the forgiving sort. He'd cradled her, kissed her, told her that everything would be alright. There was hurt in his voice, pain. He'd even paced the bedroom, uttered uncharacteristic profanity, slammed his palm against the wall. But, in the end he'd come to her, told her that the relationship was damaged, but perhaps not broken. There would be no condemnation; healing would be a difficult but worthwhile process. All he asked was the assurance that they could focus on the relationship together, as a couple. How had she ever thought this man weak?

Liberty opened a desk drawer, withdrew a few personal items: a digital camera, a stuffed monkey Seth had given her on their first anniversary, some make-up, a toothbrush. These, she put into a cardboard box situated on the floor to her right. "I know you're there, Horace." Her voice was firm though her heart was shattered. Could she truly walk away from McKenzie? Their relationship – however bizarre and unhealthy – had been of the most intimate sort. Not, physically, per se, but emotionally. Despite her newfound admiration for Seth, she wasn't sure it could be duplicated.

She felt an electric chill flit past, but nothing more. No image, no gorgeous god of sales. How absurd it all seemed now. How stupid.

"I can't do this anymore. Horace, it'll kill me."

"What do you mean, you can't? You have to. These are my clients, Liberty. This was my life and you took it away from me."

Liberty rose upon unsteady legs, and turned to face the voice. "I did nothing to you."

There was a sudden rush of wind.

Wind!

She was indoors. How could there be wind?

"Horace, I was wrong. This is not me. Not at the core. I'm not what you think."

The wind increased. Papers fluttered about the office. Liberty's hair blew across her face.

"You will not abandon me!"

"Horace, I can't keep going. The baby. I think there's something wrong with the baby."

"Do you think I care about that child? My accounts, Liberty. My people. My life! You took them all!"

Now the wind whipped about the place. A chair rolled by. A plant toppled from atop a file cabinet, crashing to the floor, shattering, sending dirt and leaves spilling onto vinyl tile.

"I didn't know. I was just trying to do a good job."

The phone on Liberty's desk rose, twirled in a clumsy pirouette.

"On the phone, Liberty. Now. Dial the phone. Sell. Sell!"

"I can't, Horace. I can't!"

The phone leapt forward, the cord wrapping around Liberty's neck despite her attempts to evade it. Tighter. It wound tighter. Liberty tugged at the snakelike cord, pulled, bit. The base of the phone slammed against her head with surprising force. Once. Twice. The world went momentarily black. Liberty fell to the floor as the swirling wind continued to increase in intensity. It seemed she had her own private hurricane.

A filing cabinet toppled. A desk spun on one leg like a top. Two computer monitors collided, sending shards of plastic and glass darting in every direction. Liberty blinked, clearing her vision. The rush of wind became an oceanic roar in her skull. Still she struggled against the demon phone. It pulled tighter, tighter, now cutting into the flesh of her neck. Dribbles of blood dampened her fingers as she tugged at the impossible noose.

Liberty crawled forward, unable to stand, her vision darkening at the perimeters. She only had seconds of consciousness left to her. After that, death. Certainly death. If she could make it to her desk drawer. Find some scissors, cut the cord.

Just as she came to within reach, Liberty's desk shuffled, scooted away, and then, rising from the floor, smashed into the opposing wall. It almost seemed Horace had plucked her intentions from her mind.

Almost.

Liberty slumped to the floor. If possible, the phone cord drew tighter yet.

There was movement. Somehow, Liberty picked it out from amidst the chaos. Someone entering the room. Horace?

No. Seth.

As arranged, Seth had come to pick her up, to take her home on this final eve. She tried to scream. Tried to warn him. With all her heart, she tried to warn him. But there was no air in her lungs. There was no voice left to carry a message over the raging gale.

Seth had only a moment to take in the scene, for his eyes to go wide, his jaw to drop, before Liberty's own desk smacked into him at what had to be seventy or eighty miles an hour.

It was over. Everything was over. All because of Liberty's ambition, her selfishness, her greed. She didn't fight it now. Her vision went gray and then black. Her last thought was of Carly, the daughter she'd so neglected. Seth's sister would take her, of that Liberty was certain. She would be in good hands. Better hands.

One last twist of the cord.

One final exhalation of breath.

And then nothing. Nothing at all.

*****

"Mr. Farris?"

Chris Farris turned, shook his head, and then spoke. "Oh, I'm sorry, officer. I'm still taking it all in. Quite a mess."

"Understandable, sir."

"I'm sorry," said Farris. "I really don't have much to add. Liberty Marks had been working late, overdoing it really. I don't know why her husband was here. Maybe he came to confront her on her behavior. She'd been acting strange, talking to herself, shouting, crying. Something was going on with her. I don't know what."

"You believe this to be a domestic dispute?"

Chris shrugged and exhaled. "If so, it was a Doozy. Look at this place. You'd think a tornado had hit. Both of them dead. I just can't believe it."

It would take days – weeks even – to restore the office to a workable condition. But, Farris went about the task with a quiet stoicism, renting a separate suite until work was completed, reassembling lost files and bids. Most of the documents were saved on computers, but some of these had been damaged beyond repair. It was a weighty task. When finally he could put it off no longer, he addressed the issue of Liberty's client list. These very special customers would need to be reassigned to someone of exceptional aptitude. It really wasn't much of a decision, he supposed. Kaminski was the up-'n-comer. He had the drive, the talent. "What do you think, Horace?" asked Farris as he stared at the blank wall across from his new desk. "Kaminski? Do you think you can make something of Kaminski?"

"Perfect," gleamed Horace. "Such ambition. So much real ambition. Not like Liberty Marks. No, much better. Oh, we'll make just the perfect team."

TOMORROW YOU KILL

It seems the most extraordinary of days can often begin in the most mundane fashion. Glenda Davis stared at her bed. It was made flawlessly, as if no one had touched it the entire night. Perfect. Like every morning. She shuffled into the kitchen – much like every morning. She set the coffee to brewing, fixed two slices of toast – whole grain wheat, none of that bleached white nonsense children eat. And she wondered why she was so tired – much like every morning. To the best of her knowledge, she'd slept well. She hadn't had a bout of restless leg syndrome since Dr. Morrow put her on that annoying little pill. But she never seemed rested anymore. Perhaps she was hitting an age where her body needed additional nutrients. "Hitting an age!" She was only just over forty. She shouldn't be "hitting an age" for another ten years or better. At least by her thinking.

Glenda sighed, poured her brew, rubbed her eyes, and moved toward the Dell computer situated atop a once tidy little desk in a nook adjacent the kitchen. She'd need to sort through those bills one of these days. It seemed things were piling up a bit more than they had in the past. Strange. She'd always been rather tenacious about organization, about timeliness, about an orderly life. She was too tired. That's all there was to it. Sigh. Maybe she had "hit an age" where she needed to start getting to bed another hour earlier each night. Barely out of her thirties and youth was already racing past her. Sometimes life really was a poor excuse for existence.

It was Arnie's fault of course.

Her ex-husband.

If he hadn't been such a pig, if he hadn't fooled around, if he hadn't left her for that bimbo whore Debbie, Bambie – whatever her name was – Glenda's life would still be on track. It would be tidy, neat, predictable – as any good life should be.

Glenda sipped fresh ground dark from her Dilbert mug and seated herself before the computer, clicking the mouse on Internet Explorer and then into Yahoo to check her email. Scanning through her inbox, Glenda found the predictable mix of clutter and nonsense. Spam. Spam. Another forward from some woman named Ruby. If all of those chain emails really worked, the woman would be a billionaire by now. More spam. It seemed no one ever sent legitimate emails anymore. Glenda couldn't remember the last time someone had actually tried to communicate with her in some genuine fashion.

But, this one was curious. The subject line read, "Tomorrow You Kill." It was sent by Selbstovna. How would that be pronounced? "Sel-bst-ohv-na," she said aloud. Curious, but most likely a prank. Glenda deleted it with a quick peck of the mouse.

She sipped at her coffee, contemplated which dress to wear to work, dazed off for a second, and then glanced again at the screen.

"Tomorrow You Kill."

There it was again. Not the same email, but a new one, just sent within the last minute. How strange.

She deleted this one as well. Some sort of spam to be sure.

Another hit of brew.

Another glance at the computer screen.

Another message with that same ominous title.

Well, this was getting annoying. Who was this Selbstovna person? And "Tomorrow You Kill." Obviously this person couldn't mean murder. That would be ridiculous. It was probably just some "killer" sale or some nonsense like that.

Glenda deleted the message yet again.

In what seemed like a second's time, another appeared.

Now this was getting ridiculous. "Okay, Mr. Selbstovna," she said aloud. "You win. I'll open your little email. But, this had better not be a virus. There are places to report people like you."

SELBSTOVNA – IN CASE YOU WERE WONDERING, YOU DO NOT KNOW ME THE WAY YOU THINK YOU DO.

Well, that was strange. Glenda sipped another hit of her coffee and responded.

GLENDA – WHAT DO YOU MEAN BY "TOMORROW YOU KILL?"

Another click of the mouse, and another seemingly immediate response.

SELBSTOVNA – LET'S CALL IT AN INVITATION.
GLENDA – WHAT TYPE OF INVITATION?
SELBSTOVNA – AN INVITATION TO KILL, OF COURSE.
GLENDA – KILL WHAT? KILL WHO?
SELBSTOVNA – KILL ME, DEAR LADY. TOMORROW YOU WILL KILL ME.

Glenda rose from her seat, paced the room. What type of insanity was this? Who was this man? What could he mean by any of this? She thought of simply walking away, or of possibly calling the police – not that that would do any good. But soon she found herself back at the keyboard. For some reason she couldn't just let this go. Yes, it was probably just some juvenile prank, but it nettled her, compelled her to respond.

GLENDA – WHAT DO YOU MEAN, "TOMORROW I'LL KILL YOU?"
SELBSTOVNA – I WOULD THINK THE MEANING OBVIOUS.
GLENDA – I'M NOT A MURDERER.
SELBSTOVNA – ARE YOU SURE ABOUT THAT? ARE YOU REALLY SURE? YOU DID RESPOND TO MY EMAIL. YOU MUST, AT LEAST, BE INTRIGUED BY THE THOUGHT.
GLENDA – NO! I AM NOT! I TRIED TO DELETE IT, BUT YOUR MESSAGE KEPT COMING BACK.
SELBSTOVNA – AND EACH TIME YOU THOUGHT ABOUT IT JUST A LITTLE MORE. WONDERED IF IT REALLY MEANT WHAT IT

SEEMED TO MEAN. WONDERED IF JUST MAYBE IT COULD BE TRUE. AND THEN, FINALLY YOU COULDN'T HOLD OFF ANY LONGER, SO YOU OPENED THE EMAIL.

GLENDA – I THOUGHT IT WAS SOME PRANK.

SELBSTOVNA – MAYBE YOU'VE WONDERED WHAT MAKES A KILLER TICK, WHAT IT FEELS LIKE TO CONTROL ANOTHER'S FATE, TO WITNESS THE LIFE DRAIN FROM THE BODY.

GLENDA – NO!

SELBSTOVNA – PERHAPS YOU'VE HELD A GUN, OR EVEN A KNIFE, AND MARVELED AT THE QUIET POWER OF COLD METAL IN YOUR PALM.

GLENDA – I'VE NEVER HELD A GUN.

SELBSTOVNA – PERHAPS YOU'VE FELT ANGER WITH SOMEONE: YOUR ABUSIVE FATHER, THAT NOSEY NEIGHBER WHO COULD NEVER KEEP OUT OF YOUR OH-SO-PRIVATE BUSINESS. OH, OR HOW ABOUT THE UNFAITHFUL HUSBAND THAT USED YOU UP AND THEN DISCARDED YOU LIKE LAST WEEK'S TRASH? OR MAYBE THERE IS NO REASON. MAYBE YOU SIMPLY SEEK AN ESCAPE FROM THE MINDLESS MONOTONY OF YOUR DAILY ROUTINE.

GLENDA – STOP IT! I'M SIGNING OFF. NEVER CONTACT ME AGAIN!

SELBSTOVNA – TELL ME, WHAT WOULD IT TAKE TO MAKE YOU KILL ME?

GLENDA – NOTHING! I'M NOT A KILLER. THERE'S NOTHING YOU CAN DO.

SELBSTOVNA – THERE'S ALWAYS SOMETHING. YOU MAY NOT REALIZE IT, BUT THERE'S ALWAYS SOMETHING TO AWAKEN THE KILLER INSIDE.

Glenda was up and away from her computer. Her brow was damp, her hands jittery. She marched into the living room and then back to the computer nook, and then the kitchen – and the nook, across to her tiny bedroom, and then back to before the accusing eye of the monitor. There were more emails. Six already. Staring. Accusing. Beckoning. She walked away again. For how long? A minute? Two? Five? There were four more emails.

Glenda took a deep breath. She had to calm herself. Had to let go of this. The man, Selbstovna, meant nothing to her. He was a stranger. A cyber-stalker, she supposed. She had to think. Had to calm down and think. She was so worked up that it seemed difficult to put two thoughts together.

Time.

What time was it?

How long had this man distracted her from the duties of her day? Nine-oh-six already. Work. She was late for work. Glenda was never late for work. Hurriedly, she rushed toward the bedroom. She'd call Morgan, her boss, while dressing. With luck she'd be no more than an hour late.

*****

The day had been long, tedious, and seemingly never-ending. Or so it seemed. Truly, it was all a blur, hardly a detail remembered. Well, she supposed, that was the type of work she did: mindless, repetitive. No wonder nothing stuck.

She hadn't thought of Selbstovna all day. Even now, as she moved to-ward her computer, he had nearly escaped her mind. A nuisance, a bother, that's all he'd been. Hardly worth the uproar of this morning.

There was another email. Of course, there was another email. This one from only moments ago. Glenda considered deleting it, but was too curious to be sensible. No, it wasn't some latent killer drive as her cyber-stalker had suggested, but this whole thing was bizarre, and the unusual always had a way of drawing attention.

She clicked the mouse.

The email opened.

SELBSTOVNA – I'M SO GLAD YOU FINALLY CHOSE TO READ THIS EMAIL. YOU'LL WANT TO TUNE IN TO THE SIX O'CLOCK

NEWS. ANY CHANNEL WILL DO. I'M SURE YOU'LL FIND
SOMETHING OF INTEREST. YOU MIGHT EVEN FIND IT
MOTIVATIONAL.

Glenda glanced down at the clock toward the bottom right corner of her
computer screen. It was six-oh-three. The news had just started. She hesitated, contemplating the idea of ignoring the request altogether. But ultimately,
curiosity got the better of her. She hated being manipulated. Arnie had been
the king of it. But still, this was an unusual circumstance. If she disregarded
the summons, she'd be wondering what it was that she'd missed for weeks to
come. Better to play along and be done with it.

A strange thought occurred to her then.

Arnie.

The great manipulator.

Could it be...?

No. Arnie simply wasn't that bright. If Selbstovna had been Arnie, there
would have been numerous misspellings and grammatical inconsistencies.
Even the name, Selbstovna, hinted at a linguistics background beyond
Arnie's meager capacities. Curious, she hadn't heard from him in several
weeks now. She wondered where he had holed up.

The television sprang to life. Glenda maneuvered away from CNN and
landed on channel five, the local CBS affiliate. She turned up the volume to
listen to the announcer.

"...*alerted by an anonymous call, the police found the young woman's
naked body hanging in the abandoned storefront on the forty-three hundred
block of North Kirkland. Stuffed in the woman's mouth was a note reading,
Tomorrow You Kill.*"

Glenda's heart leapt into her throat. Her stomach reeled into a roller-
coaster dive to her bowels.

"The police have not yet released the victim's identity, but they have assured us that due to the condition of the body, this was most definitely a murder and not a suicide…"

Brenda dropped the remote. It bounced unnoticed on the beige Berber carpet. "No, no, no, no," she repeated. "No, no, no." This could not be. These things could not be connected. It was impossible that she'd been involved in an ongoing dialogue with a murderer.

"…Police officials have asked that anyone having information concerning this crime should call the Aptera Police Department at 671…"

"No! I will not believe this!"

This couldn't be. She led an orderly life. Everything in its place. Routine built upon routine. No chaos. No disorder. The thought that anything diabolical could cross the threshold of her being seemed so alien as to be ludicrous.

Glenda paced, right, left, right. She kicked something with her foot. Something hard, not heavy. The remote. She'd kicked the remote. Bending, she picked it up, flipped the channel to NBC. There it was again: the same crime scene, a different reporter. Click. ABC. Again, the same scene.

This was not real. This could not be real.

The police. She should call the police.

To what end? She knew nothing. Not even the killer's name or location. Selbstovna was not a real name. This much was obvious. What could she offer? Nothing. If anything, she might direct suspicion upon herself.

Almost unconsciously, she found that she was once again seated before her computer.

GLENDA – TELL ME YOU HAD NOTHING TO DO WITH THIS.
SELBSTOVNA – ARE YOU READY TO KILL ME YET?
GLENDA – TELL ME YOU DIDN'T KILL THAT WOMAN.
SELBSTOVNA – I'M A KILLER, NOT A LIAR. ARE YOU READY
YET? ARE YOU READY TO KILL ME?

What was this man thinking? Why Glenda? Why was she being drawn into all of this?

GLENDA – NEVER! I'M GOING TO THE POLICE. I'LL TELL THEM WHAT I KNOW.

SELBSTOVNA – AND WHAT DO YOU KNOW – GLENDA? YES. GLENDA. I KNOW WHO YOU ARE, BUT YOU COULD NEVER ADMIT TO KNOWING ANYTHING OF ME. NOT YET, AT LEAST. AND DO YOU KNOW WHAT ELSE I KNOW, GLENDA? I KNOW YOU WON'T GO TO THE POLICE. YOU CAN'T. AND THAT'S A VERY, VERY POWERFUL THING TO KNOW. DON'T YOU THINK?

Worst of all, he was right. Glenda couldn't go to the police. Well, she could, she supposed, but what real information did she have to offer? Emails from a stranger. His unsubstantiated claims of involvement. No. She needed to talk with this man, reason with him. Though, reason and logic seemed very alien commodities just then, still, that must be her approach.

Glenda gazed down at the keyboard, sought to steady her hands. Breathe. Just breathe. She just needed to relax, to take her time.

GLENDA – WHY ARE YOU DOING THIS TO ME?

SELBSTOVNA – DEAR, DEAR, GLENDA. I'M JUST TRYING TO GET YOU TO STOP ME FROM DOING THESE HORRIBLE THINGS TO SO MANY OTHERS.

GLENDA – YOU DON'T HAVE TO DO THESE THINGS.

SELBSTOVNA – YES, I DO, GLENDA. I REALLY DO.

GLENDA – WHY?

SELBSTOVNA – IT'S WHO I AM.

GLENDA – THEN, SEEK PROFESSIONAL HELP.

SELBSTOVNA – YOU KNOW I'VE TRIED THAT. YOU KNOW IT DIDN'T WORK. I DON'T WANT TO BE A MONSTER. I DON'T WANT TO DO THESE THINGS. SOMETIMES, I JUST GO AWAY TO

SOMEPLACE DIFFERENT IN MY HEAD. I PRETEND THAT I'M NOT A KILLER; THAT I LEAD A NORMAL, MUNDANE LIFE. BUT, I AM A KILLER, NO MATTER HOW I TRY TO DELUDE MYSELF. THAT IS WHY YOU MUST KILL ME, GLENDA. KILL ME SO THAT I CAN FINALLY STOP KILLING. I'VE DONE SUCH A TERRIBLE AMOUNT OF KILLING.

GLENDA – LET ME CALL THE POLICE. THEY CAN STOP YOU.

SELBSTOVNA – NO. NOT THE POLICE. THIS NEEDS TO BE BETWEEN THE TWO OF US.

GLENDA – YOU SAID YOU'VE SOUGHT HELP IN THE PAST. MAYBE A DIFFERENT THERAPIST, MAYBE DIFFERENT MEDICATIONS. THE GOWEN NEUROLOGICAL INSTITUTE IS ON THE EDGE OF TOWN. THEY HAVE SEVERAL PSYCHIATRISTS ON STAFF.

SELBSTOVNA – DON'T MENTION THAT PLACE! THEY DO THINGS IN THERE. THINGS TO YOUR MIND. THINGS THAT CHANGE A PERSON. NO. THERE WILL BE NO MORE DOCTORS. NO MORE DRUGS. THE ONLY WAY YOU CAN HELP ME IS TO KILL ME. DO THIS ONE THING AND FREE ME FOREVER.

Glenda blinked. Her head ached. Her arms and legs trembled. This was too much. What he was asking, it was far too great a price. She could not follow through with Selbstovna's line of reasoning. There must be another way.

Glenda's eyes returned to the computer monitor. There was another message. Almost absentmindedly, she opened it.

SELBSTOVNA – IT APPEARS I NEED TO BE MORE PERSUASIVE. THE TEN O'CLOCK NEWS. WATCH IT AND KNOW THAT YOU COULD HAVE PREVENTED WHAT YOU SEE.

GLENDA – NO, SELBSTOVNA. YOU DON'T HAVE TO DO THAT. THERE'S ANOTHER WAY. LET ME HELP YOU.

Glenda clicked the mouse, sending the message. She waited. Where previously, the mysterious Selbstovna responded almost immediately, in this instance, Glenda sat staring at the screen for what seemed several minutes.

GLENDA – SELBSTOVNA! TALK TO ME. DON'T DO THIS!

Glenda rose from her seat. "He's not responding. He can't do this. He can't keep killing."

She crossed into the kitchen, grabbed the house phone, staring at it, contemplating a 911 call. She should do it. She should make the call. Who cared if they thought her crazy? It was the right thing to do. Even if no one acted on her information, at least she'd know she'd done all that she could.

But, no. She couldn't. She knew she couldn't. What could she tell the police? What really could she tell them? None of this made sense.

Aspirin. She needed aspirin. Maybe something stronger. Something. Anything. This had to stop. This just had to stop.

*****

"A sixteen year-old girl was found murdered today, just three blocks from her home. As with the murder of Deborah Cordich who was found earlier today, the girl had a note stuffed into her mouth, reading, 'Tomorrow You Kill.'"

Glenda clicked the remote. The television screen flickered and then went black. He'd done it. Selbstovna had killed another one. And now the police were looking at other unsolved murders, suspecting that though there were no notes left at these previous crime scenes, that other evidence pointed toward the same killer. If possible, Glenda sank further into the couch. Somebody had to do something. Somebody had to stop this monster.

Not somebody.

Her.

Glenda.

She had to stop him.

The killer had asked her to do as much.

How he had selected her, she didn't know. Was this someone she knew in life? A coworker, a neighbor, an old high school flame? Arnie? There must be some connection somewhere. She couldn't accept that she had simply been some random selection. That would be just too much. Things like that didn't happen in her life.

Her life was orderly.

Her life was tidy.

She was methodical.

Everything she did had purpose.

Everything was part of a plan.

Glenda rose. Her legs quivered ever so slightly as she made her way to the computer and logged on. The keys seemed, cold, stiff, lifeless. Just the same way Glenda felt. Nothing would ever be simple again. Nothing would be as it had been.

GLENDA – SELBSTOVNA, WE NEED TO TALK. WE NEED TO MEET.

She inhaled deeply, closed her eyes, allowed her fingers to rest on the keys. When she opened her eyes, a response sat waiting.

SELBSTOVNA – HAVE YOU FINALLY DECIDED TO KILL ME?

GLENDA – I'VE DECIDED TO MEET YOU.

SELBSTOVNA – ONE COULD VERY WELL LEAD TO THE OTHER.

GLENDA – NOT NECESSARILY.

SELBSTOVNA – I MAY BE SOMETHING – OR SOMEONE – ENTIRELY DIFFERENT THAN WHAT YOU EXPECT.

GLENDA – LISTEN, I'M ONLY DOING THIS BECAUSE I DON'T FEEL I HAVE ANY OTHER CHOICE. PLEASE, NO MORE GAMES. JUST TELL ME WHEN AND WHERE TO MEET YOU.

SELBSTOVNA – THE PLACE WHERE I KILLED DEBORAH CORDICH MAKES ABOUT AS MUCH SENSE AS ANYTHING, I SUPPOSE. THE NORTH SIDE OF THE BUILDING, NEAR THE LOADING DOCK. YOU KNOW THE PLACE, I'M SURE.

*****

Glenda pulled the blue/gray sweater closer about her, hugging herself in the cool night air. She could hear traffic in the distance. Meridian Boulevard was no more than three hundred feet distant, yet somehow it seemed a light year from where she stood. Every sense was attuned. She heard the crunch of gravel from beneath her as she moved slowly forward. She smelled the lingering stench of recently-laid asphalt from beyond the nearest building. She felt the fluctuating breeze nettle her cheeks. It seemed the shadows moved, that they slowly, ever so slowly closed in around her. Why had she done this? Why had she come? What could she really hope to accomplish?

Possibly, she could accomplish getting herself killed.

An unnerving thought hit her then. Perhaps that was it. Perhaps this was how the killer lured his victims. Had Deborah Cordich, or that other young girl been lured in a similar fashion. Did this Selbstovna surf the net, sending out random emails, waiting for a response, manipulating a meeting such as this?

It was possible, she supposed. More than that, it suddenly seemed quite likely.

Glenda glanced left and then right. She pivoted, gazing back toward her tiny yellow Smart car. Where was he? Where was Selbstovna?

"Selbstovna is here."

Where had that voice come from? Why couldn't she see him… or her? Was that a feminine voice? "I don't see you," she said, still scanning the shadows.

"Just keep moving forward. Selbstovna is never too far."

But, she didn't move further forward. There was no need.

"You're Selbstovna. It's…" She hesitated, attempting to focus on the gray/black shadows wavering in the halogen light. "You're not what I expected."

"Is anyone ever really what we expect? Though, I have wondered why you assumed me to be male. A helpful delusion, perhaps. A means to add yet one more degree of separation."

Squinting, Glenda pressed her fingers against her forehead, massaging her temples. "I don't understand."

"Do you really want to understand?"

Of course she didn't want to understand. Wasn't that what this was all about, her unwillingness to accept her current reality? "Understand what? What is it that I don't understand?"

No! Don't ask that question. Run! It's not too late to run.

"Understand who I am. Who you are."

"I… I'm not sure what you mean."

The voice was warm, reassuring. Familiar. So very familiar. "Think about it, Glenda. There was a time, not so long ago, a time when you were an academic. You studied European culture and language. Think about the name, Glenda. Think about Selbstovna. What does Selbstovna really mean?"

Glenda stared forward into the shadows. She knew this. She did know this. Or, at least, she'd suspected it. The languages. She'd recognized the roots. "Selbst is German for 'self,'" she said. Though the words were soft and hesitant. "Ovna is a Russian suffix meaning 'of,' or 'daughter of.'"

"Yes," coaxed Selbstovna.

"So, Selbstovna would mean, 'of self,' or 'daughter of self.'"

"You understand then?"

"You're saying that I am you. That I am the killer."

"Oh, yes, Glenda. Selbstovna has done so very much killing. And that is why you must kill Selbstovna. For the sake of all those others yet to be killed."

Glenda's heart leapt. Her vision seemed to pulse light to dark to light. "But, that means killing myself. You want me to kill myself."

"No, Glenda. *You* want to kill yourself. That's why you've created me. You needed some help; a little extra impetus to push you forward."

"But, I don't want to die."

"Did your victims want to die, Glenda? Did that young girl want to die?"

That girl! That filthy slutty girl. That tramp!

"She… always made fun of me. She trampled across my lawn, made out with her boyfriend behind the shed – where I could see them from my kitchen window. She was disgusting!"

"And the others? There were so many others over so many years. Arnie suspected, you know. It's why he left you." Selbstovna was closer now. There was so little distance. So little separation.

"Harvey Wetzel was a crook! He conned me into buying insurance I didn't need. He… put his hand on my knee. And… Debbie Cordich stole my husband, seduced him – that's why he left me! For a tramp. He left me for a tramp. Margaret Samson! Oh, speaking of tramps, Margaret Samson deserved nothing but disease and death."

"Oh, I'm sure they all deserved it. But, so do you, Glenda. Surely you must see that."

Glenda stomped the gravel-covered ground, slammed her fist against her right thigh, surely causing a bruise. "No!" she screamed, again slamming fist to thigh. "It was you! Not me! You! You're the one! You're the killer!"

"Yes, I'm guilty. I must die. And therefore, so must you, Glenda. You did bring the knife, I assume?"

"Yes, but…"

"The same knife you used to kill Deborah Cordich."

"Yes."

"Then, you know what to do. I'm sure you know just what to do."

Glenda stared directly ahead. Straight into the place she imagined Selbstovna to stand. She allowed the knife to slip from her hand. It offered a subtle, clank/clatter as it struck the rocky ground. "Yes," said Glenda, a more determined tone inching into her voice. I know exactly what to do."

It was then that the first hint of a siren could be heard. It was distant, originating from the north. But, there was no disguising that it drew nearer with every moment. Glenda smiled. Not a full smile. Not even a sad smile. Simply, an expression of resolve. "You see," she said. "The killing really must stop. I meant it when I said I would never kill you. I meant it when I threatened to call the police. I did so upon arriving to this spot, just before stepping out of the car to confront you."

"No."

"We will both survive this night, Selbstovna. Both of us. Me and myself. And though you're some twisted part of me, you'll never again taste the blood that drives you."

Glenda could feel the panic race through her form, could hear the quiver in the voice – her own voice – as Selbstovna sought to regain control of the situation. "You're wrong, Glenda! You'd wrong! I'll still be with you. And as long as I am, you'll know there's a killer in you. You'll kill again. You must know that. You'll kill again."

Again, Glenda smiled. This time it was of a more genuine sort. "No, I don't think so. You see, I've just defeated you. I didn't know that's what I was doing when I called the police. But, I understand now. I've taken away your control of me and transferred it to the hands of others. You may still be within me, but you'll never be free again."

With that, Glenda turned facing the approaching police cars. She would tell them. Tell them everything. They would lock her away, yes. But there would be no more killing. Glenda simply could stand no more killing.

She took a step forward, paused, looked to behind her. There lie the knife. So many killings. So many. She turned around, bent, clasped the cool wooden handle. Perhaps, she'd best bring this as well. One never knew. It might come in handy.

THE DEATH & FURTHER ADVENTURES
OF BENJAMIN BRICK

The day that Benjamin Brick died was one of the few days that he didn't think about death. It wasn't that Benjamin was obsessed with the subject; it was just that he considered the matter quite frequently and with quite a degree of curiosity. He often wondered what it would be like to know the day of one's own demise, to have that foreknowledge, to be able to say, "Well, no. Tuesday won't work. You see, I'm going to die on Monday. Do you have plans Sunday? Sunday I'm free." He wondered what it would be like, being here on earth one minute, and being in the great beyond the next. He wondered what mental gymnastics the brain must play on a fellow leading up to those traumatic last moments.

Benjamin's lifelong friend and onetime college roommate, Wade Barber, was convinced that Benjamin had a death wish. The fact that Benjamin had actually built and, then lodged in the living room, his own coffin, only confirmed the conclusion. But, what Wade failed to understand was that Benjamin held the firm conviction that no one else would build a coffin to his exact specifications – i.e., a small refrigerator, Wi-Fi connection, and Sudoku puzzles etched on the inside, just on the off shot that Benjamin's burial was of the slightly premature variety.

Now, it might seem that someone who desperately wanted to know the hour of his own death well in advance of the event might be suicidal; seeing as suicide is one of only two ways a person can actually know in advance the hour of his death. (The other being execution; and Benjamin Brick was in no way the type to land on death row. Not, at least, unless rolling stops became punishable by death. Benjamin loved his rolling stops.) But no, Benjamin was not suicidal. In truth, he hoped that he would just know of his impending doom through some supernatural informant or gut instinct. He hoped there would be a tingle on his flesh or a shiver deep within his spine. Or maybe he hoped he'd hear the voice of the reaper while it was still a ways off, possibly asking directions to Benjamin's slightly smaller than midsize studio apartment.

Despite Benjamin's rather persistent desire of foreknowledge, he was actually thinking of sherbet when death descended upon him. The rainbow variety. He hadn't had it since he'd been a boy, but this day Benjamin had a taste for rainbow sherbet. He wanted to experience the tingling sweetness on his tongues, to feel the treat slowly melt as it slid down his gullet, giving him shivers all the way. And if death hadn't so rudely intervened, he might have had one last taste of this childhood treat.

The vampire wasn't tall. In fact he was several inches shorter than Benjamin, who stood only five foot eight inches. He wasn't imposing: youngish, perhaps twenty to look at him, rather scrawny, with a bad cowlick, and a rather pronounced zit on his forehead. Benjamin, with his ample belly and fleshy arms, probably outweighed him by thirty pounds or better. And seeing as Benjamin didn't believe in vampires, the creature just wasn't all that frightening. Truly, his first thought was that here was a guy who needed to spend quite a bit more time in the sun and even more time in the shower. The man, thought Benjamin, smelled more or less like week old liverwurst.

"Hello," said the vampire as he appeared as if from nowhere.

"Oh! Hello," said Benjamin who was marching steadily up Market Street in hopes of arriving home in time to catch the latest episode of Dr. Who. "I don't have any money to give you," he added, assuming the young man to be seeking a handout.

"I don't want money," said the vampire in a voice that reminded Benjamin of the comedic actor, Jon Lovitz, albeit, with a very stuffy nose and a mild dose of helium.

"Ah! Good!" nodded Benjamin. "As I'd said – I have none." Benjamin made as to move around the vampire.

"I would, though, be quite interested in a few pints of your blood," said the Jon Lovitz-on-helium vampire as he again blocked Benjamin's way.

"Ah!" nodded Benjamin. "You're with the Red Cross. Well, I'd most certainly consider making a donation, but needles and blood are two of my least favorite things. Less so even than rutabaga."

"No, no, no," said the vampire. "Perhaps this will help to clarify matters." The short, rather unimpressive creature rummaged about his pockets for a moment and then produced a rather dusty and worn business card which he handed to Benjamin.

AMOS BEXLEY

VAMPIRE

Sustaining Member of the National Association for the Advancement of
Vampiric Individuals

Est. 1492

"Established 1492?" asked Benjamin with a wry grin and a subtle chuckle.

"There was more to Columbus than history records," nodded the strange character with a knowing wink.

"Right. And you claim to be…"

"A vampire," said the vampire.

"Uh-huh," grunted Benjamin with a nervous grin. "Of course you are. Well, I hope that's working for you – odd hours, I suppose." Benjamin then proceeded to walk around the scrawny little vampire, thinking that crack cocaine sure made people do weird things.

Five paces later the vampire was in front of him again.

"I have fangs – see?" said the vampire, who seemed terribly intent on impressing Benjamin.

"Hmmm, nice," said Benjamin, noting the two, thin, pointy teeth. "I'm not a dentist, but I'm sure something could be done with those. Gotta go."

"No. You may not go," shot the vampire, his voice becoming higher yet, nearly a full-fledged squeak. "I am going to bite you."

Benjamin rolled his eyes. "No offence, but have you looked at yourself lately?"

The vampire paused, cocked his head, and then offered a rather toothy grin. "Well, no. We vampires have a bit of a problem with mirrors. I'm sure you've heard."

"Well, you're not exactly imposing. Why don't you just go form a cult or something?"

The scrawny vampire stepped closer yet, his eyes fixed on Benjamin's neck, his rather pronounced odor causing Benjamin's nose to burn an itchy stuffy burn. "I'm going to bite you," he said with a generous grin. "And then you're going to die and become a vampire yourself."

And then he did just that.

Benjamin couldn't have guessed that the small, sallow-faced young man with the too-big nose and strangely red eyes could move so fast, but here he was, his rather squishy mouth firmly clenched against Benjamin's fleshy neck.

And, there was pain.

Oh, yes there was pain. But it was of the strangely tingly sort. And suddenly Benjamin's brain flooded with bizarre alien images. He would later learn that there was often a mental connection made at these times, that the victim would somehow visit the memories of the attacking vampire, that an indelible bond was often created, that the soon-to-be vampire might learn the wisdom of the ages, or witness events of monumental significance. Such was not the case with Benjamin. This vampire's history was not quite so grand or compelling. Though the images that invaded Benjamin's waning consciousness did lead to his rather peculiar last words as a living breathing human being. "Is that a horsey?" he asked before falling dead to the concrete.

And then there were images.

Strange…

    Strange…

        Strange…

            Images.

*****

The vampire Amos Bexley's pivotal event occurred somewhere in the late eighteen hundreds. Or, perhaps it was the seventeen hundreds. Maybe, the sixteen hundreds, but no earlier than that. The vampire's recollection was a bit sketchy on dates. Still, historical context aside, the events which Benjamin witnessed as he floated blithely within the vampire's mind are as follows:

Jeremiah, Obadiah, and Amos Bexley were of a rowdy sort. All three, still in their early twenties, single, and with far more than a little time on their ever-restless hands, seemed to have adapted mischief as a sort of ad-hoc religion. On this particular summer's eve in the late sixteen, seventeen, or eighteen hundreds, they had just made off with Mrs. Carney's Shetland sheepdog. As well, they had released the sheep that the stolen pup had been charged with maintaining. The sheep, being of a rather stupid sort, ambled about listlessly, mucking up the lawn and dining on Mrs. Carney's prize petunias.

Mrs. Carney, the county's only school teacher for at least the past one hundred and fifty years, was not quite pleased with these developments and ran, clothed only in a pink and white knit house dress, shouting shrill classroom-appropriate curses at the giggling lads. "Dang-gone-nibblers, give me my darn-lolly precious little Shetland puppy," she cried. "Give me my precious little Shetland puppy!"

(It might be noted at this time that Mrs. Carney only held class well after sunset and had a strange aversion to Italian cuisine.)

The Bexley boys never knew the dog's true name – if, in fact, it had one. This was how the woman always referred to the panting little beast. "Come here, my precious little Shetland puppy. Sit, my precious little Shetland puppy. Don't do-do on the petunias, my precious little Shetland puppy."

But seeing as the dog snarled and snapped at Amos as he carried it off in the crook beneath his left arm pit, none of the Bexley boys thought the dog to be the least bit precious.

As such, they disposed of it properly.

The dog was last seen strapped to the back of a renegade mustang pony, galloping off into the western landscape as the dog yapped and growled. Obadiah would forever claim that he heard the thing cry, "Dang-gone-nibblers," as the young steed made its way over a distant knoll, but Amos considered the claim fanciful.

Jeremiah, Obadiah, and Amos were fond of a local watering hole, called, "The Watering Hole." The actual title of the place was "McKinney and Brewster's Excellent Refined and Mostly Non-Lethal Beverage Emporium." But all agreed, this was a bit of a mouthful, and so, "The Watering Hole" it was.

After the my-precious-little-Shetland-puppy incident, the lads were understandably parched, and thus retreated to their favorite source of libation. Here, they laughed, giggled, flirted with the young women of the county, and basically proceeded to get rather sloppily plastered. As the evening progressed, the boys began to realize that in the past three years they had caused just about all the mischief they could cause without graduating to something truly criminal.

This was a dreadful problem. What were they to do with themselves? They'd used up all of their tomfoolery and were smack out of tricks.

"We could rob a bank," offered Obadiah as he removed his index finger from his ear, and then examined it for mysterious treasure. "That's plenty mischievous."

"They could hang you for that," snapped Amos in a voice that would one day resemble that of actor Jon Lovitz. "This isn't the twenty-first century where the penal system simply incarcerates criminals for a specified sentence and then lets them out on good behavior." (Amos was always speculating on what life would be like in the twenty-first century. If there had been such a thing as science fiction in his day, he would have won a Gene Roddenberry award, except, that is, for the inconvenient fact that Roddenberry had yet to be born.)

"How do you know that's how they'll do it in the future?" asked Obadiah with a smug cock of the head and a knowing twist of the lip.

"Don't listen to him," chimed Jeremiah. "He don't even know how they do it now."

"Ah, but I do," said Amos, now settling in as if to lecture. "They execute felons because the Federal penitentiary system has yet to be established. As such, they have no place to house habitual miscreants." Amos was no more educated than the other boys, but he'd found a battered old Oxford dictionary on a muddied path one Sunday afternoon and had taken it on as his most constant companion.

"They got jail," offered Jeremiah.

"Jail's for detaining inebriated oafs, not for incarcerating hardened criminals for an extended duration."

"Doesn't matter. We're not robbing a bank."

They all shrugged. Obadiah sipped at his drink. Amos clucked his tongue. Jeremiah attempted eye contact with a rather cute, but exceedingly married young woman in the south-east corner of the room.

"How about we string a pig up from a tree?" offered Obadiah.

"Pigs are too heavy," said Amos.

"We could trick Miss Sweetwater into thinking we're doctors and get her to take off her top," leered Jeremiah.

"The only people believe you're a doctor would be... nobody," said Obadiah. "Besides, Miss Sweetwater's got to be ninety years old. (In reality, the lady in question was thirty-six, but Obadiah was close.)

"How about we pour beer in the town well?"

"Done that."

"We could neuter farmer Atwater's cattle."

"That too – twice."

"How's about we pickle Dorothy Pruitt's daffodils?"

"If you're looking for some real mischief, you could become creatures of the night, you dag-nobble-bip-knockers."

Yes, it was Mrs. Carney. Sometime after one a.m., she'd strolled into the Watering Hole and found the boys sitting at the bar, mulling over their dim future prospects and contemplating ear wax. Her too-curly hair hung in ill-defined clumps which spilled across her mildly symmetrical face. Her right eye seemed to gaze past Jupiter somewhere, while her left eye stared hypnotically at the young miscreants. Her knuckles cracked, her knees popped, and she smelled of week-old liverwurst. Offering Jeremiah and Amos a nod and a wink, she squeezed between the two, settling at the bar.

"I said you could become creatures of the night – a vampire," she repeated with a none-too-well-disguised grin. "The ultimate piece of mischief for the most mischievous boys in the land."

"Vampires commit murder. Murder is not mischief; its felony, Mrs. Carney," said Amos.

"Yep," agreed Jeremiah as he leered at the woman's not-insubstantial bosom. He'd found her attractive since the second day of second grade. Though, in truth, Jeremiah found almost every woman under the age of three hundred fifty nearly irresistible.

"We'd be hung," added Obadiah.

"Yeah, because they don't got no penis system yet," added Jeremiah with a smug nod.

"Penal system," groaned Amos as Jeremiah stared blankly in his direction.

Mrs. Carney shook her head slowly, ever so slowly. "No, you would not," she said with all the authority of a well-entrenched schoolmarm.

"I fail to see why not," said Amos with a bit of a scholarly huff.

"Because vampires have special supernatural abilities. They work beyond the boundaries of human law."

The Bexley boys all stared at her as if her Jupiter eye had just performed intricate calisthenics.

Mrs. Carney's smile inched just a notch nearer her cheeks. Her strangely sharp teeth glistened.

"That's stupid," said Obadiah.

"We have no desire to become nonexistent mythical creatures," added Amos with an authoritative air. Though, Benjamin read in the memories that his curiosity had already been piqued.

"Don't dismiss the idea so quickly," said the vampiress. "Think about the fun you might have."

"Fun?" asked Jeremiah.

"Of course," said Mrs. Carney, a gleam in her best eye as she leaned forward as if to share a profound truth. "Who are the best pranksters in the county?"

"Well, us, of course," said Obadiah.

"And, what would be the ultimate mischief for a master prankster?"

"Obviously," said Amos. "You're suggesting that becoming vampires would allow us a profound freedom in tomfoolery."

Mrs. Carney smiled her mischievous grin. "Not only could you prank this town out of existence, but you could live forever."

"Even into the twenty-first century?" asked Amos. For, more than anything, Amos longed to see the twenty-first century.

"Ah," grinned Mrs. Carney, her fangs now fully revealed. Unfortunately, dental floss had yet to be invented, and so the sight was more gross than horrifying. At least to Amos, that is. Jeremiah and Obadiah, sloshed, smashed, and inebriated as they were, somehow had sense enough to scream, holler, and flee for their lives. Amos, though, leaned closer yet, a strange twinkle in his narrow eyes.

"Curious. Very curious. I think you might just be telling the truth."

"I am," said the murderous madam.

"And I could live into the twenty-first century?"

"I don't see why not. Just avoid garlic. It plays havoc on the digestive system."

And so Amos Bexley became the vampire that would one day create yet another vampire, this one named Benjamin Brick.

*****

Benjamin awoke with a start. He'd been plagued with bizarre dreams of a time long ago and strange people and events that in no way meshed with his particular view of reality. His room was strangely dark – and stuffy. Had he forgotten to crack the window? And why was his mattress so stiff? This did not feel like his Posturepedic.

Reaching up to scratch an itch on his forehead, his hand thumped against what seemed to be a wooden obstruction. Curious. He reached to his right. Apparently, there was a wall. Above him, the same. To his left? Yep, there too. It was at this point that he started to scream. For now it all came back to him: his encounter with the slightly, but not quite dead Amos Bexley, the attack, the weird mental connection. This was not good. This was not good at all. For Benjamin Brick was a man of several phobias and foibles previously not heretofore discussed in this volume. To the point:

A) He was a claustrophobic.

B) a vegetarian.

C) He was quite a bit more than a little afraid of heights.

Seeing as vampires sleep in a confined space, drink a distinctly non-vegetarian variety of blood, and turn into bats in order to soar high above the city, Benjamin was not quite suited for this new life, or, death as it were. At this particular moment, claustrophobia was the primary irritant, which, as it turned out, then exasperated Benjamin's asthma. Benjamin was really quite upset, for he realized with some trepidation, that not only did his mother not bury him in the coffin he'd so carefully prepared for just such an occurrence, but she didn't even have the decency to bury him with his inhaler. Mother would definitely need a strong talking to.

So, Benjamin screeched, he howled, he hammered on the coffin's lid until his hands were raw.

Nothing.

Trapped.

No way out.

And who'd have thought that vampires could have such horrible asthma? Shouldn't he have left that behind with his former life? Shouldn't, at the very least, he be given a free pass on earthly ailments?

Go figure. Hollywood had it all wrong.

After perhaps an hour of toddleresque tantrums, Benjamin settled into a depressed calm. He was a vampire. An actual vampire. The undead. Curious, he slipped a finger between his lips. Yep. There they were – fangs. Rather sharp too. Really, this was simply unacceptable. Here he was, all fanged up and no place to go.

And truly, how was he expected to get out of this stupid coffin? It wasn't like someone had been kind enough to install a latch on the inside – not like the one Benjamin had built!

But, obviously, other vamps managed to exit their coffins. How was it they did this?

It was at this point that Benjamin took a deep breath, attempted to bring his asthma under control, and began detailing what little he did know about vampires:

They bite people. That was a given. Obviously, the whole vegetarian thing was out the window. They don't like garlic. Too bad, that. Garlic is actually quite good for the heart. They had the ability to turn into bats. That, Benjamin supposed, cut down on airfare. But, Benjamin was afraid of heights. He never flew anywhere.

Ah! It hit him then. They can turn into mist.

He could turn into mist and escape this teeny-tiny, dark, shrinking, coffin.

Ok.

How exactly was that to be done?

Benjamin tried snapping his fingers. Nope. He tried singing "Play Misty for Me." Nah. Stupid idea. He tried calling upon the spirit of the mist. Apparently, there was no such thing. Couldn't someone have at least left him a Vampires for Dummies book?

Finally, he decided it best to simply concentrate on the task.

Mist. Mist. Mist.

Mist. Mist. Mist.

Mist. Mist. Mist.

And suddenly – and rather amazingly – he was mist.

And just as suddenly, he was standing on muddy ground staring down at his own tombstone.

And then – not so amazingly – he was kneeling on that same ground, vomiting on his own grave.

Turning one's body into mist, he found, was not a pleasant experience.

It took Benjamin a few moments to gather his rather unstable wits and take in the scene. Yes. There was his grave, still freshly settled, the tombstone not yet damaged by age and elements. "Benjamin Brick," he read aloud. "Beloved brother and son."

Huh!

His mother hadn't even had the decency to mention three-time employee of the month.

That woman!

And then, as if from a lightning bolt, in a wave of sudden fury, he was hungry.

But this wasn't the, "Let's run down to the nearest vegetarian hamburger joint and pick up a veggie burger" kind of hungry. This was more of the, "I need human blood – now!" variety.

Benjamin's stomach twisted. His bowels contracted. Sweat poured from his brow. His vision blurred and then sharpened.

Was that a man over there?

A human being?

A blood-filled human being?

Yes, yes. It was the groundskeeper. How very convenient. Benjamin could use a nice tasty jugular about now. He took a step toward the man. And then another. He felt his fangs lengthen in anticipation of the warm, juicy, living...

Okay, that was just plain gross.

Truly. How had he managed to think such thoughts?

Despite the rather tumultuous gyrations of his screaming belly, Benjamin turned away. No, no, no. This was not who he was. This went against everything he believed. He had to find a way out of this, had to do something.

But, the groundskeeper smelled so tasty. Mmmmm, maybe just the tiniest...

No! Benjamin stomped his foot. No!

Sweat beaded on his brow. His nostrils flared as he breathed in the groundskeeper's musty scent. His stomach jumped and hollered. Benjamin had to leave, had to flee this place before giving in to that oh so tempting temptation.

Benjamin didn't so much decide to turn into a bat, as he just did it.

And oh, did his acrophobia kick in as he soared unsteadily above the sleepy town.

Bat vomit, anyone?

*****

Benjamin squatted on Wade's window ledge, perched there like a pigeon on a statue, clinging to the wall with all his might, and looking anywhere but down – a long, long way down. Wade was a monster junkie, a "B" horror movie fanatic. He was an expert on all things undead. Wade knew things. Benjamin was sure that Wade could help with his little vampire predicament.

"Wade! Let me in," screamed Benjamin, his eyes averting the ground, his fingertips raw from clutching the tan and red bricks about the window. "Wade! Now would be a good time!"

When finally, Wade ambled into the room, he was wearing pajama bottoms only and carrying the latest issue of Fangoria magazine. Pressing his face against the glass, he squinted.

"Benjamin? Aren't you supposed to be dead? I went to your funeral. Kinda brought me down."

"Yes, Wade. I'm dead. Now may I please come in?"

A curious grin creased Wade's face as he squinted just a bit more mightily, his shoulder length blond hair spilling onto his nose, his cheeks crinkling. "Aren't you afraid of heights? I'm on the eleventh floor."

"Yes, yes, I'm deathly afraid of heights. Will you please let me in?"

Wade stood upright and stepped back three paces. "The window's unlocked."

"No, you need to invite me in. I'm a vampire. I can only come in if you invite me. Stupid rule, really."

Wade's grin grew broader yet. "A vampire? Are you gonna bite me?"

Benjamin sighed an exasperated sigh. This was getting ridiculous. "Wade, I'm a vegetarian."

"Well, okay. But, don't eat my fichus."

A tug on the window frame.

A rather awkward tumble through the window and onto the floor.

And Benjamin was face-to-face with his best friend.

"Okay, out with it. Let's see the fangs."

Benjamin sighed, rolled his eyes, and opened wide.

"Ooo! Those are nasty."

"Yeah, tell me about it. I have no idea how I'm going to floss."

Wade crossed the room and tossed himself onto the couch. "You're wheezing. Asthma still a problem?"

"You have no idea."

"Figures. Hollywood got it wrong again."

Benjamin paced left, then right. Wade's jugular looked particularly tasty just then. "Listen, Wade, I need your help. We've gotta figure something out."

Wade thumbed through his magazine pausing on a page featuring a particularly buxom female vampire straddling a coffin and beckoning to the camera with a curled index finger. "Your type?" he grinned, displaying the page to Benjamin.

"Wade, I'm serious."

"Okay, I'll bite. Get it? I'll bite."

"Wade!"

"Okay, okay. What's the problem?"

Benjamin rolled his eyes. "Really? You've gotta ask?"

"Oh, yeah. Vampire. Got it."

"Wade, I'm doing everything I can right now not to bite your neck and suck you dry."

Wade nodded, still studying the girl in the magazine. "Well, I'm off limits, but, have you tried your address book?"

"What?"

"You hang out with some real loony tunes. Who knows? Maybe some girl will let you bite her. You might even get a date out of the deal."

"Wade!"

"Trust me. It'll work."

It didn't.

For some reason, no one wanted to be bitten by Benjamin the vegetarian vampire. Though, there was one girl, Margie, who claimed that if Benjamin were ever to be alive again, she wouldn't mind going to a movie sometime. To this, Benjamin exclaimed, "Being dead stinks!"

Wade responded by nodding and handing Benjamin a bottle of Old Spice.

Benjamin crossed over to the window and gazed down upon the city. His stomach tightened further, and it was all he could do to keep himself from launching across the room and taking a hefty bite out of the much-too-relaxed-for-the-situation Wade. "I guess I'm going to have to do it," he said after long moments of contemplation.

"What's that?" asked wade as he studied a photograph of a scantily-clad female zombie.

"You, know. The whole evil vampire thing. Go out. Find some stranger. Bite her on the neck."

Wade shrugged. "I'll get my coat."

*****

The night had turned cool and damp. A subtle breeze breathed a bitter breath from the east. Foot traffic was sparse except for the occasional hooker or drug dealer. Few cars traversed the street. It was well past midnight and the town belonged to those who thrived on the underside of human activity. They stood on the corner of Market and Main, Benjamin scanning the few passers-by for potential victims and Wade eyeing the mostly malnourished-looking, hookers. "How about her?" asked Wade, indicating a particularly skeletal girl in a short leather skirt and a stained and yellowed tube top.

"Too scrawny. How much blood could she hold? I don't want to kill her."

"What about him?" asked Wade, indicating the burly bouncer standing just outside a club entrance. "He's got to have a couple of gallons."

"He'd break me in two."

"Aren't you supposed to have super strength or something?"

"Nope. Hollywood got that wrong too."

Wade shook his head in disgust. "Next, you're gonna tell me that all vampire chicks don't have forty-five double D's."

"Wade, I've got a need here."

"Yeah, yeah. Take a hit on your inhaler. You're wheezing."

Benjamin did as instructed and followed as Wade made his way across the bustling street. "Where are we going?"

"I had a feeling you'd have problems with this, so I figured we'd check out Renfield's. It's a vampire club."

"Vampire club? They have vampire clubs?"

"Well, not for real vampires. At least, I don't think so. It's where all the weird Goth vampire wannabes hang out. There's gotta be someone in there hot to be bitten."

As expected, the club was dark. The walls were of deep red velvet (similar to the interior of Benjamin's coffin). The music throbbed. Strobe lights pulsated disjointedly in opposition to the mind-numbing beat. The place was small enough to feel crowded, though there were probably less than fifty people in the entire establishment. Most huddled in small groups, sipping various crimson-colored drinks and displaying plastic fangs. Everyone wore black, had faces birthed in Clorox, and lips of Bing cherry, all pouting and forlorn. As a point of fact, Benjamin was the least vampiric-looking person in view.

"This is awesome," drooled Wade as he eyed an anemic girl wearing leather shorts that might possibly cause a string bikini to blush. The Maybelline bite marks on her neck were smudged, which somehow added to Wade's excitement.

"This is so wrong," offered Benjamin. Though, he had to admit, the scent of all of those blood-filled bodies did create a certain stirring within.

After nearly an hour, no mingling, and three awkward encounters with a rather odiferous middle-aged waitress named Mina, Benjamin finally decided that a young waif of a woman, off in the far corner, was the most suitable target. This, because she wore a fur shawl, and as a vegetarian, this irked Benjamin to no end.

"Finally," said Wade as he eyed his watch. The night had gone on much too long, and Wade had found the Goth chicks less than hospitable.

"But what if she says no?" asked Benjamin, a slight tremor to his voice. Need aside, he was still none too thrilled with the prospect of taking a hearty bite out of a fellow human being.

"Alright," said Wade through an exasperated groan. "Any more of this and I'm through. You come knocking on my window just when I'm getting ready to settle into a long night of B-rated DVD heaven. You tell me you're a vampire. Do I freak? No. I try to help my good buddy Benjamin. But, this is getting ridiculous. You either bite someone or you don't. But, I've gotta be at work nine AM tomorrow and this is going nowhere."

"Okay, okay. I get it. I'll go bite the fur lady."

He approached slowly, assessing the woman as he puffed his inhaler. He studied the black rings painted beneath her eyes, the smudged red lipstick, the disgusting fur draped about her delicious too-white neck.

Unfortunately, for Benjamin, the things he didn't observe were those of paramount importance. I.e., a small can of mace, a ten pound handbag, and bony knee poised to deliver a swift jolt to a rather delicate portion of Benjamin's anatomy.

In short, Benjamin's first vampiric attempt was a dismal failure.

Bruised and bloodied, Benjamin hobbled toward Wade, not noticing the short, scrawny figure sitting beneath an Anne Rice poster until the creature spoke in his ever so Jon Lovitz way. "Well, I'll have to admit," said the vampire. "That was just about the most pathetic attack I've ever seen. Wait'll the vampire counsel hears about this. You'll never get tenure."

Benjamin's eyes went wide. His fangs grew long. His finger quivered as he pointed at the not-very-impressive form before him. "You! You did this to me. You killed me and turned me into this... this thing!"

"Wait a minute," said Wade as he stepped to beside his buddy. "Him? This little weasel? He's the vampire that bit you? Why didn't you just smack him with a fly swatter?"

"Oh, you're one of those," said the vampire, now rising from his coffin-like bench. "I suppose you think all vampires need to look like a teenaged Twilight heartthrob."

"Yeah, yeah. Zip it. Listen, you turned my friend into a vamp. He's an acrophobic, vegetarian, asthmatic, who likes to eat garlic on just about everything. This just isn't going to work."

The vampire Amos Bexley shrugged. "Well, I don't know what you want me to do about it."

"Listen, I'm guessing you've been a vamp for a while. In all of those years, you must have come across some way to reverse the process."

The vampire seemed to contemplate for a moment. "Well, no. Nothing comes to mind."

"Nothing. No loopholes. No chants. No eye of newt or liver of squirrel?"

Amos shook his head in the way one might do to an overly persistent two year-old. "Of course not. If there was, don't you think I and most every other vampire would pounce on it? I mean, you have to admit, being a vampire does have its drawbacks. Before chat rooms, we had no social lives whatso-ever."

"Yeah, I really feel for you. Now, about Benjamin. You saw him. He's not going to make it as a vamp. I mean, my aunt Matilda with her gout is more frightening."

Amos shook his head. "I'm sorry. There's simply nothing I can do. Once a vampire has ingested his first blood, well, the deal is sealed."

At this, Benjamin perked up. Had he heard correctly? Had Bexley said what he thought he'd said? "First blood?" asked Benjamin. "I haven't ingested any."

Amos seemed perplexed at this, perhaps a bit taken aback. "What about the groundskeeper? I made sure there was a groundskeeper on hand for when you exited your coffin."

Benjamin screwed his face in disgust. "The groundskeeper? Gross. I can't go around biting people just because they're handy."

"But, that's what vampires do," protested Amos Bexley.

"And that's exactly my point," said Wade. "Benjamin is never going to be a true vampire. He doesn't have the stomach for it."

Bexley nodded. "Yes, yes. I see that now. But, still, the chance of reversing vampirism, even if successful, it's not pleasant."

"And biting people is?" shot Benjamin.

"Ah, I see your point," said Bexley with a bit of a jackal's grin. He squinted his eyes, scrunched his lips, and then said with a nod, "There's still one possibility. But I'm going to need a certain salve and a special potion. But, first. A coffin. Does anyone have a spare coffin lying about?"

*****

Amos Bexley was suitably impressed that Benjamin had a coffin waiting at the ready in his apartment; but he couldn't quite fathom his claustrophobic reticence to climbing inside. Wasn't laying in a coffin the most natural thing in the world? After all, virtually everyone spends the better part of eternity doing just that.

Finally, after much deliberation, a shouted declaration or two, and Wade's assurance that he'd watch out for Benjamin's best interest, Benjamin climbed in. "How could I ever have found this so fascinating?" he asked as he laid his head on the too-small pillow.

"That's what I've been asking for months, you freak," smiled Wade. "Though, I've gotta admit. It kinda suits you."

At this moment, Amos Bexley stepped forward, smiled down at Benjamin, and said, "Night, night," as he moved to shut the lid.

"Wait! Wait!" screamed Benjamin. "What are you doing? You know I suffer from severe claustrophobia."

"Well, right now, you suffer from severe vampirism. And unless you do as I say, that condition will become permanent."

Benjamin glanced at Wade, who nodded and said, "I've got your back. Go ahead."

And so it was then that Amos Bexley closed the lid on Benjamin Brick.

There was no light. Not one miniscule iota of even the thought of light. Even after the merest of seconds, the air seemed to stagnate, to thicken, to catch in Benjamin's throat. Inhaler in hand, he sprayed three puffs, drawing them deep into his lungs. "What do I do now?" he gasped through a constricted larynx. He knew he couldn't last more than a few minutes. Already his skin was creeping every which way, his head was pounding, and his toes itched something fierce.

"Hmmm, how about you hum Beatles songs backwards," came Bexley's muffled voice.

"What?" asked Benjamin and Wade simultaneously.

"Just kidding," said the vampire, who, even after all these years, was a prankster at heart. "You seemed like the type that would fall for it."

"So, now what?" Benjamin heard Wade ask. "You said something about a salve and a potion."

"Oh, I did, didn't I? Well, none of that will help," said Bexley. "I just said it to keep him calm. Really, he's stuck. If I was you, I'd find a good lock, wrap the coffin in garlic, and keep him in there indefinitely. One of these days he's going to bite you. Just a matter of time. Mark my words."

Benjamin's heart leapt in terror. He pushed against the lid, but couldn't get his arms into a decent position to gain leverage. He shook, rattled, gave an honest shove.

"You mean there really is no way to cure him?" came Wade's voice from some distant place.

"Well, one, I suppose. Since he hasn't yet tasted blood, he would be cured if the vampire that made him were to be slain."

A pause.

And then a groan as Bexley realized what he'd just revealed.

If the vampire that made him were to be slain!

There was hope. Slim, but still...

Benjamin threw his weight to the right, then to the left, right again, left again. The coffin began to rock. "Wade," he yelled. "Don't let him get away!"

Right. Left. Right.

He felt the thing start to shift on its platform.

Push. Shove. Push.

Crash!

Benjamin spilled out onto the floor as the hinges to the coffin lid popped like holiday firecrackers. "Wade! The closet. Camping gear."

"Got it," said Wade, understanding immediately what Benjamin was going for.

As it seemed, so did Amos Bexley. Fangs bared, the scrawny vampire lunged toward Wade, only to be intercepted by Benjamin the vampire bat. He flitted about the vampire's head, dodging, darting, screeching. Anything to distract the creature while Wade dug through the closet.

"Dude, do you ever throw anything away?" hollered Wade as he tossed a bruised and battered Hardy Boys book onto the carpet.

"Squeak, squeak, squeak," replied Benjamin. Translation: hurry up!

Bexley backhanded Benjamin, sending him crashing into the wall with a resounding *thump*! And a rather pronounced squeak.

No! The vampire was upon Wade now. Teeth bared. Claw-like fingers curled. All was lost.

And then the wooden tent stake was in Wade's hand. The arm came down.

Bexley's eyes went wide. He screamed something about the blessed twenty first century as the stake found its mark. Within seconds, his body had turned to dust.

Hollywood got that one right.

Upon Bexley's demise, Benjamin fell immediately to the floor.

No longer a bat.

He was...

He was naked!

How did he get naked?!

And so it was that Amos Bexley came to his end on a crisp summer night sometime after the beginning of the twenty-first century.

Benjamin recovered completely, or so he said. But, forever onward his friends noted his new-found affinity for raw meat and attractive necklines. He would lead a very, very long life – and keep very odd hours.

FORTUNES OF A LESSER SON

Richard Renfro crossed the hated threshold but progressed no further. He simply stood there, just within the room, alternating his gaze between his feet and a defiant hangnail on his left thumb. When finally he ventured a glance toward the desk, his gaze was not returned. Lillian was writing something, longhand, in broad sweeping strokes, and seemed not to notice Richard's presence.

"Well, Richard," she said after several agonizing moments. "You insisted on seeing me, out with it."

Richard wasn't quite sure how to begin. He'd made the decision to come here, yes. He'd determined in his mind to follow through. He'd even rehearsed the words he'd for so very long, planned to speak. But, now that he was here, now that it was time, Richard had no words to offer, no forceful oratory, no grand proclamation. Richard, if truth be told, had nothing.

"Richard?" she prodded. "You look stupid standing there fiddling with your fingernails."

Suitably chastised, he took one step forward, and chanced eye contact. "Um, this might take a while. Mind if I sit?"

"I don't have time for a lengthy conversation, Richard. Either say your piece and leave, or set an appointment for a more appropriate time."

Something clicked inside Richard. Something of the anger, the venom, the hate that had welled inside of him for endless years. He had been dismissed for his entire life. He'd been shoved aside, made to feel unworthy, lowly, undeserving. But, it was not he that was undeserving. It was not he who should grovel or beg. It was not he that should quake in fear every moment, every hour. Somewhere, somehow, Richard reached within himself, and slowly, softly, almost inaudibly, said, "No."

Lillian appeared almost amused as her pen paused in mid stroke. "Excuse me?"

Another step forward. A defiant gaze. "I said, no, mother. I'm here now. We'll do this now."

Lillian chuckled as she set her pen aside and leaned back casually in her high-back leather chair. Her Kelly green eyes twinkled as her glistening wine-colored lips curled into a sly grin. "Well, the rabbit has teeth, does he? Then I suppose you should sit. You look flush just standing there like a frightened mongrel. I wouldn't want you to pass out and drool all over the new carpeting."

Richard nodded and stepped forward. It seemed his momentary infusion of courage had fled like a frightened cur confronted with a yapping pack of pit bulls. Stumbling slightly, he sank into the diminutive seat opposite his mother. As always, she was impeccably dressed. A smart jade top, silk with subtle wisps of black and tan, helped to highlight her cat-like eyes. Her red hair seemed never to change, to never alter in style or length. Her complexion was pale yet vibrant, her posture, even when relaxed, appeared proper and forceful. She wore no wedding ring – there was no need – and what little jewelry she bore was tasteful and understated, yet, clearly of great value. "Well, speak up, Richard," she said with a bit of a snit. "As you may have noticed, I'm busy."

Richard cleared his throat, glanced up toward his mother and then down again as he picked at the errant nail. Just one sentence. That was all. Just one sentence and the thing would be set in motion.

"Richard?"

"I've…" Richard hesitated. "I've come to bring an end, mother."

There. It was out. There was no turning back. He would be forced to explain. Forced to confront her with all that he knew. Forced to suffer whatever consequences she saw fit to impose.

"What was that, Richard? You're mumbling like a schoolboy."

"I've come to bring the end," he repeated, this time more forcefully.

Lillian leaned forward, resting her forearms on her desktop. She appeared thoroughly amused. "The end? You've come to bring the end of what?"

"I've come to bring the end of this, mother. All of this." With that, Richard spread his arms, indicating all that was about him.

"Well, the rabbit really has come out of his hole, hasn't he?"

"What you've done will come to light, mother." The adrenaline flowed now, boosting Richard's resolve, or at least, allowing him little pause to fret and contemplate.

"What I've done?" Lillian chuckled. Clearly, she was enjoying this.

"The bank," said Richard. "Father, the Braymer family. Even Kenneth."

Lillian swiveled her seat, offering Richard a profile. She stretched her legs out comfortably, one crossed lazily over the other. She had the legs of a thirty year-old – or so she claimed – and loved displaying them, even when the only audience was her own son. "Everything is rather all-encompassing, Richard. What is it that you believe you know?"

"Suspect, not know."

"Suspect. Only suspect?" Lillian sounded far too amused for Richard's waning comfort. "Oh, your brother Kenneth never would have dared confront me with nothing but suspicions. That, I suppose, is just one of many ways that Kenneth was superior to you."

Richard was up now, pacing the room, staring at the antique bookcase, glowering at the parchment and mahogany world globe, anything but making eye contact with Lillian. "Maybe I do know," he said. "Maybe I always have. Not through any evidence. Not really. Just in my bones."

Lillian's hearty laugh nearly caused the trembling Richard to leap. "Your bones! And what do your bones tell you now, Richard? Are they telling you to quit, to leave this too-comfortable life of yours; to flee the position, the title, that you know you'll never achieve elsewhere? Or, maybe your bones are telling you something more. Are your bones telling you to somehow eliminate me, to try some mad power play, or worse?" Here she paused, cocked her head to the left, and released an uncharacteristic snort. "No. Nothing so severe. One would need a spine to contemplate actions of that magnitude."

Richard was speechless. Every word had fled, every thought evaporated.

"Am I a devil, Richard? Is that how you see me, a devil in need of punishment?" Again, she laughed, now sitting upright, facing forward, drawing Richard's unwilling gaze into those piercing green orbs. "Am I a devil, Richard? Your brother, Kenneth, thought so. But, he's no longer here, is he?"

Enough! He'd heard enough. His threshold had been met and exceeded far too many times. "I quit, mother. I refuse to work for you any longer. To have anything to do with any of this."

"Is that how you intend to bring an end to me – by quitting? Oh, you poor delusional boy. What you do for me, well, certainly I'll have the position filled by noon." Lillian smiled, readjusted herself in her seat, and picked up her fourteen carat pen. "Now, if you'll please excuse me, I've a meeting for which to prepare."

Richard marched forward, to only inches before the desk. His hands quivered near uncontrollably, and so, in order to prevent himself from clasping them together in a show of fear, he pressed each palm down onto the surface of the desk, a strangely powerful-looking move, he thought with some subtle humor. "I know things, mother. Horrible things. I can bring you down."

Lillian waved her hand absently, dismissing Richard's attempt at strength. "Of course you can, Richard. Now, go scurry away like a good little rabbit."

"This is not over, mother."

Lillian smiled a practiced piranha's smile. "Oh, no. It most certainly is not over."

*****

Richard loosened his hold on Emily and gazed at her through tear-streaked eyes. She'd recognized his pain as he'd walked in the door and had immediately rushed to comfort him. Her blue eyes were sharp, intelligent, gauging his every nuance, as she studied his features. Though, late into the day, her hair was perfect, her make-up fresh, her energy undiminished. How Richard wished he shared her verve for life and all of the trials and pitfalls that accompanied its journey.

"I don't know, Emily," he said after a moment. They'd been at this, it seemed for hours, hugging, talking, revisiting the same issues. "It was as if I was nothing to her. That all the work I've done is meaningless. All those hours I put in, the nights I didn't even make it home."

Emily drew in breath, hesitated only momentarily, and then spoke. "That's your mother, Rich. She has no soul; she just devours whatever she pleases. Look what happened to Kenneth – your own brother. We'll never know the truth of that."

The truth of that.

Sometimes Richard wondered if there even was such a thing as truth. And if there was, did he really want to become intimately acquainted? Some truths were just too troubling to confront. There were truths that could alter a life, endanger it even. Perhaps these were things better left alone, better left to the past, where all is nothing, and nothing is all that there ever will be. The past, as horrid as it might be, was at least a thing gone by.

Richard blinked, attempted to bring himself back into focus. Emily was talking, saying something about Lillian, of how she destroys everything she touches. Disengaging from his wife's embrace, Richard nodded agreeably and, pacing the teak floor, began to pick at his fingernails.

"Richard, focus. Listen to me."

"I'm here, Em. I'm listening."

Emily stared at Richard, her face was stern, Concern etched her brow as she stepped forward in an effort to gain his full, unhindered attention. "Something needs to be done about her, Rich. Something drastic. She's dangerous. You know that. Think about your father. Think about your brother."

But Richard didn't want to think about his father. Lillian had maneu-vered the man not only out of their marriage, but out of all his business holdings, and then right out of the state. Richard could only imagine what horrible blackmail had been employed. Even more so, Richard didn't want to think about his brother. Kenneth. The favored one. If Kenneth, the golden boy of the family, could be dealt such a cruel fate, what would befall Richard – the rabbit – the lesser son?

So many times, Richard went to Kenneth's bed, stood beside him, gazing down on his inert form. How he wished his comatose brother could communicate. How he wished he could offer guidance as he had in the past. Would he agree that mother should be dealt with? That she was out of control, dangerous even?

Presumably so.

Wasn't it these beliefs that put him in this position to begin with? Wasn't it his willingness to confront Lillian that cost him his life?

Oh, there was no proof. Nothing that could be tied to Lillian. But was proof truly a necessity? How was it that Kenneth's accident occurred only hours after he'd confronted Lillian concerning the missing Braymer family? How was it that Kenneth's laptop computer, containing all of his documentation, all of his proof about her illegal business dealings, about blackmail, extortion, even murder, how was it that this was never again seen after the accident?

How was it that Kenneth had yet to see Lillian shed a single tear for her fallen son?

Who was this woman on the inside? How could someone become so ruthless and uncaring? What drove her?

Money, of course. Lillian loved the finer things.

And power. Lillian thrived on power.

But were these enough?

Were these superficial things all there was to his mother's soul? Did she have no human connection? No love? Not one breath of compassion? Or had she suppressed these things for so long that they died withered and black, never watered, never nurtured, never brought into the light?

Was it possible for the soul of a living person to die? Could one blithely deceive loved ones and still claim to harbor love? Or did the deceit so corrupt the heart as to make it forever unloving?

Oh, how Richard wished he had Kenneth's wisdom. How he longed for his brother's temerity, his strength, his will. How he wished simply to see his smile and to hear Kenneth call him a nerd.

He would never have any of these.

Not ever again.

No, Kenneth was out of the picture. Everything now rested on Richard.

The rabbit.

The coward.

*****

It was sometime after 7 pm when the phone vibrated. Richard glanced at the caller ID and contemplated allowing it to go into voicemail. But, he was preconditioned. Even now, Lillian had a hold on him. Thirty-two years old and still he cowered beneath mommy's cruel stare. He truly was a pathetic thing.

Lillian did not offer a greeting as Richard brought the phone to his ear. She didn't ask him how he was doing or offer any apologies for her behavior nine hours before. She simply said, "I have need of you this evening."

Richard rolled his eyes and then closed the heavy door to his study. Emily would be furious if she knew he was talking with Lillian. "Mother, we've been through this. I no longer work for you."

"No, of course you don't, Richard. Now, I need you to run an errand."

"Mother, I…"

"I may no longer employ you, Richard, but I did birth you. One little run for your mother won't hurt anything."

And that was the end of any debate. Lillian gave Richard an address, told him when and where to be, made sure he'd taken the information correctly, and then the phone was dead.

Just like Lillian's soul.

Just like Richard would be if Emily learned that he had already fallen back to within his mother's influence.

He felt sick. Nearly nauseous. This could not continue.

And yet it would. He saw no other option. No other out.

Emily was waiting when Richard arrived home from his errand. She sat at the dining room table, a collection of photographs spread out before her. Somehow, he'd known this would be the case. Mother worked quickly when riled.

Richard had known it was a set-up from the moment the woman had answered the door. Candy, she'd called herself. There stood Richard, supposedly picking up a package for Lillian, and the woman – barely more than a girl, really – answered the door in a scant, black negligee. The negligee had come off as soon as she'd pulled Richard through the doorway. He'd resisted, of course. But still she'd managed to wrap her naked form about him, to lock her lips to his neck and pass her hands over his most private parts. All for the benefit of an unseen camera. The frightened young man had fled not more than a minute after entering the home, but that meant nothing, he knew. Mother had won another round. She'd scored another point in separating Richard from Emily, in driving them apart.

Lillian had never cared for Emily. Perhaps she'd thought her career as a pharmacist too lowly to be connected to the family. More likely, she didn't like the competition for Richard's loyalties. Emily was an independent thinker – much like Lillian – and this, Lillian could never forgive. Lillian's lesser son had never once refused her, had never thought of defying her will, not until he'd "hooked up with that tramp." Ever since, Lillian had moved to distance the couple from one another. Until now, her maneuvers had been nothing more than an irritation.

Richard approached the table and glanced down at the glossy photographs hot off the laser printer. A masterful job in such a short amount of time, really. There was a closely cropped shot: his own head, the girl sucking on his neck, her bare breast exposed. Nowhere was it evident that he resisted the advance. Another showed Richard from behind and the naked girl facing him, her negligee heaped on the floor. The photograph made it look like a planned rendezvous, like Candy had been waiting for Richard, her lover, to escape his wife for a brief escapade.

"Emily, I didn't..."

She cut him off, not allowing him the opportunity to explain. "We've got to do something about your mother. Look at this. She's attempting to frame her own son. She's trying to make it look like you're having an affair."

"So, you understand?"

Emily dropped the photographs to the table and angled her head toward Richard. "Really, Rich, you? I'm sorry, Hon, but you don't have the courage to have an affair."

Richard stared down at his fingers as they twitched and pulled. He would have felt better if she'd said she trusted him, that she knew he'd never contemplate such a thing.

"She's manipulating us," continued Emily. "She's trying to regain control of you. And I'm afraid that if something's not done, if you do anything else to break her hold on you, that you'll end up like Kenneth."

Richard chanced a look into his wife's eyes. Blue, like sapphire. Determined. Concerned. "I'm no real threat to her. I don't think I'm in any danger yet."

"Don't you get it? You've opposed her. That makes you a threat." Emily shifted in her seat so that she could face Richard eye-to-eye. "Think about it, Rich. She's bribed police officials. She's bedded the mayor. She has too much control, too many people willing to fulfill her twisted wishes in return for money or power."

Richard nodded. He'd heard this argument before. He knew the accusations, knew his mother's history. "But, Emily, everything we have is circumstantial. We have no actual documentation that she's done any of this."

"But, we know, Rich. We know what she's done. We know her capacity for survival."

Richard pulled out a chair, sat down at a right angle to her. "But, there's nothing we can really do. Not until we can prove something."

Emily sighed, dropped her head. It seemed she struggled with some deep internal turmoil. "Rich, I'm scared. She's always hated me; she's never shown you any respect. Now that she knows we're on to her, I don't think she'll let it go. She doesn't know that we have no proof. She doesn't know what we've uncovered."

Richard slipped his hands to under the table, hiding them as he fidgeted. "So, what are you saying we should do?"

Emily was now the one showing nerves. She was up, out of her seat, pacing the room, avoiding eye contact.

Richard rose, went to her, wiped a tear from her eye and then cradled her in his arms. "Emily, what is it? What are you thinking?"

"I'm thinking that it's kill or be killed. My God, Rich, I think we have to kill her."

*****

Richard sat staring at his comatose brother. The room was private, the hospital exclusive. But, none of that really mattered. Kenneth was unaware of his surroundings. He had been for over six months now. Ever since the freak accident that had sent his car through the guard rail and into a ravine. But, Kenneth should not be lying here. By all logic, he'd sustained only minor injuries. Nothing that should have spurred a prolonged coma. But here he was, eyes closed, inert, for all practicality, dead. Sure, the chest still rose and fell. The temperature still hovered around 98.6. The heart beat. The bowels moved. But, Kenneth was gone. He'd died that day. There was really so little point in continuing this charade.

And yet Lillian insisted that he be kept alive.

Why?

As some ongoing reminder of the power she wielded? Some living proof that she had control even over life and death? Richard could never understand his mother's motivations. She seemed such a walking contradiction. At once she could be controlling, manipulative, nearly evil in thought and deed. And in another moment she could be, not loving, no, never that, but loyal, perhaps. Or, at the very least, aware of her family and her obligations to them.

But this was seldom and long ago.

More frequently, she was cold hearted. And in truth, it seemed this was Lillian at her core. Cold. Unmoving. Willing to do anything and everything to get her way.

The Braymer family.

Bill Braymer had been a trusted employee, one of Lillian's inner circle. But, he'd apparently tried to maneuver himself into a controlling interest in the company, potentially costing Lillian millions of dollars. Not only did Braymer disappear, but his entire family had as well – all six of them. Poof! Gone.

No serious investigation followed.

This was in likelihood due to Lillian's intervention with the mayor. She'd actually had an affair with the mayor and then blackmailed him with the deed, threatening to expose her own affair to his wife and constituents. Sure, she claimed innocence, that there had been no affair, no wrongdoing, but Emily had found proof. Digital photographs and the blackmail letter. Unfortunately, this documentation disappeared before Emily could forward it to authorities. Emily had been threatened on her way home that day. Threatened with her life.

She'd remained strangely quiet for days, fearful even. When finally Richard had coaxed the story from her, she'd revealed that any further interference could lead to "unfortunate circumstances."

And now Richard was in the crosshairs as well. They were both in danger. And Richard had no options left. If not for himself, then for his wife. He couldn't allow Emily to be further damaged because he had not had the guts to make a stand.

No. Emily was right. Richard was going to have to kill his mother. He was going to become like the woman he despised in order to be rid of her threat.

He rose, approached his lifeless brother, laid his head on Kenneth's chest, and wept.

*****

In truth, the plan was quite simple. As Emily had supposed, Lillian had not yet notified security of Richard's new status as a former employee. In all likelihood, she expected him to come crawling back like a wounded puppy, begging forgiveness, and promising undying loyalty.

The thought had crossed his mind.

Could he really do it? Could he really kill someone? His own mother! Could he kill his own mother?

Manipulative – yes. Dangerous – absolutely. But, to kill her!

If only Emily had been able to hang onto those photographs of Lillian and the mayor, if only she still had the blackmail note. But, Lillian had moved quickly. Too quickly. Emily hadn't had time to make copies or to forward them on. She hadn't even had the opportunity to show them to Richard before she'd been attacked.

No. Emily was right. There was no proof. And the reason there was no proof was that Lillian was smart. She didn't leave evidence behind. And when she did, she cleaned up swiftly and effectively. And if Lillian was willing to do what she'd done to Kenneth, well, Lillian was a threat to their very lives.

He was outside of her office now. It was after hours, which meant that the staff, including the receptionist, had gone home. Lillian would still be at her desk, though. She was always at her desk till eight, often nine o'clock. Richard did not carry a gun. Emily had feared that Richard would be too nervous walking past the security guard while bearing a weapon. But, Lillian had a gun of her own. It was hidden on the bookcase, top shelf, far left, behind several large tomes that, though quite valuable, likely had never been opened.

Lillian's own gun, placed cleanly against her own head. To all appearances, suicide.

Richard couldn't have come up with this plan on his own. His brain simply didn't work that way.

A deep breath. A momentary bout of panic. One last glace at the exit. And then Richard's hand was on the doorknob. How he had the strength to twist the handle, to pull open the door, he didn't know. But somehow he had, and now he stood before Lillian, each gazing into the other's soul.

"Hello, mother," he said, noting the quiver in his own voice.

Lillian appeared tired, exasperated, as she tapped something into her desktop computer. "What is it now, Richard? I hope you're not going to whine about that whole Candy business. She probably could have done you some good, helped you to relieve some of that tension you carry about like a badge."

Richard remained at the threshold, his feet seemingly glued in place. "Mother, I... Tell me what happened to Kenneth. The truth. I need to know or else..." He paused, not knowing how to continue. "I just need to know."

Lillian turned from her computer to give Richard her full attention. "Your brother? You already know what happened to Kenneth. It's just a shame it couldn't have been you instead."

Richard ignored the dig. He'd heard these before. Emily said it was part of Lillian's power trip, part of her manipulation, a means of keeping him off guard and under control. "I know the official story of what happened to Kenneth," he said. "But, I can't ask him what really happened. So, I'm asking you. What did you do, mother?"

Lillian appeared utterly amazed at the accusation. Such an amazing actress. "Me? You think I did that to your brother?"

Richard managed a step forward. It wasn't courage he felt. No. He was far too terrified for that. But there was anger, rage, indignation, a fury birthed in a lifetime of injustices. "Don't play with me, mother. We all know what you're capable of. Kenneth confronted you that night, tried to bring you down."

"He was the one I loved, Richard."

"He knew, mother. He knew about it all and he was going to expose you."

Lillian's eyes seethed as they bore into Richard. "Yes, he thought he knew things. But, I showed him where he'd been misled."

"Lies, mother! All lies."

Before Richard even realized he was doing it, he'd marched across the room, thrown a dozen books to the carpeted floor and retrieved the cold, gray Glock revolver from the shelf. Emily had instructed him on how to use it, how to make sure that the safety was off, how to determine that there was a round in the chamber. These he did quickly, mechanically, not allowing himself to pause for contemplation.

Even now, Lillian seemed almost amused. "My gun? What do you plan to do with that?" she smiled.

"Tell me, mother! What did you do? Toxicology reports were inconclusive. The injuries sustained in the accident should not have led to deep coma. Something was done to him after the accident to keep him quiet. What did you do?" This last sentence he screamed. The gun was pointed toward Lillian in both quivering hands. As instructed, he held it in both hands. He would be nervous, likely to drop the gun or misaim. "Hold the gun with both hands," she had said. "Fire true."

"Maybe you should ask your wife," said Lillian, still seemingly nonplused by the threat to her life. She didn't think he could do it. She thought him a coward, a rabbit. "Ask Emily about Kenneth. She's a pharmacist. She would know just how to induce coma."

"That doesn't even make sense, mother. Kenneth's been comatose for months. If someone was drugging him, it would have shown up in his lab results."

"And yet you accuse me of the same." Lillian paused, gazing into her son's frightened and enraged face. "Richard, think. Just stop and think. Why have I kept your brother alive? Why have I insisted on continued life support when by all logic he's gone? Because I'm trying to determine just that. What has he been given? What has Emily used to induce coma?"

"Don't try to confuse me, mother. I will shoot."

"Oh, my dear boy, I'm not the one confusing you. There's another far more competent in that area than I."

Richard was upon her now, gun pressing against Lillian's temple. Powder-colored make-up smeared on the end of the barrel. "Don't you try to shift the blame on this!" he hollered. "You know what you did."

"Richard, take that gun away from my head."

An order. She actually still had the audacity to give him an order. "What did you do, mother?"

"Richard, you were always so easily deceived. Everything is not as you might think. I tried to warn you about that woman. I tried to tell you…"

"WHAT DID YOU DO?"

A subtle grin on wine-colored lips. Not even a flinch at his outburst. "You're just a scared little rabbit, Richard. Put that gun away before you hurt yourself. Perhaps, you, Emily, and I should have a conversation. I'm sure it would be quite enlightening."

"Mother! Give me a reason not to pull this trigger."

Lillian snorted derisively. "You're a rabbit, Richard. You don't have the stuff of a killer. You're doing this at another's insistence. Who really decided that I must die? Who first uttered the words? Who detailed the plan?"

He could not let her do this, could not let her nettle him with doubts. Not now. Not when he'd come this far. "Mother, I'll do it. I swear, I'll do it."

"It was Emily, wasn't it?" Her voice was calm, her expression smug. "And you're afraid to go home until you've played your part in her little plan."

The gun quivered in his hand. It was slippery with sweat. Even the cold metal seemed to scream at him, to accuse him. "Mother, don't!"

"You're pathetic, Richard. Worse than a rabbit. You're a puppet and you don't even know it."

"I will, mother. I will!"

Lillian settled her gaze on Richard. There was understanding, even acceptance in her eyes. "Yes, you will, Richard. I see that now. You have no choice. No will of your own. Once, you lived under my thumb, and now you're Emily's stooge. Think, Richard. Think. Who is the truly evil person in all of this? Who is really pulling your strings?"

"Mother, I can't."

"Think about the mayor. The blackmail. Who supposedly found the video, the note? Who was it that really slept with Mayor Cline? Who really stood to gain?"

Richard's hands quivered. It seemed the gun fought to leap from his grasp.

"And the Braymer family. Who benefited from Bill Braymer's disappearance? You did. And by extension, Emily. You moved into his position, took his salary."

"Liar! You're a liar and a manipulator. You always have been."

"One does what one must do to survive – to thrive."

Richard pushed the gun harder against his mother's temple, fighting to maintain control, to not drop it or flee outright. If only there was a way out. If only there was a way change this course. "Give me one reason to walk away!" he bellowed. "Please, give me a reason."

"I've given you several. But, you've been programmed not to believe."

"Mother, I'm going to pull the trigger."

"Yes you will, Richard. It's your only hope of survival. She won't wait for your inheritance to come naturally. She's too ambitious."

"Mother, I…"

"I know, Richard. The puppet must do what the puppet must do." She paused, glanced up at him, her Kelly eyes as sharp and firm as ever. "Do it now, Richard. This tension really does wear on me."

And Richard obeyed his mother's final command.

*****

They were in the limousine, Richard and Emily, after just spending nearly three hours with corporate lawyers. There were so many details, so many nuances to running the family business that Richard had never considered. His head ached. It ached most days now, the only change from day to day being that the pain got continually worse.

Glancing down to his left, Richard flicked a switch, raising the partition between the back seat and the driver. "It's interesting that they ruled it a suicide," he said, not making eye contact, but rather gazing absently out the window. "I was, after all, seen leaving the building."

Emily shrugged, and pulled her chinchilla shawl over her right shoulder. "You got lucky," she said. "You should have been more careful."

"But, why didn't they question me? And why was the mayor there? He shouldn't have been involved in the investigation."

Emily rolled her eyes. Annoyance crept across her sharp, beautiful features. "Just be thankful, Rich. Everything went our way."

Richard scoffed. "Yeah. Imagine that."

They sat in silence for perhaps another three minutes, each absent the other, each engrossed in thought. At long last, Richard angled toward his wife, studied her lovely face, tried to determine if he really knew her at all. "She said some things," he said.

"Who?" It seemed she was nearly surprised that he'd bothered to speak. It seemed even more so that she was annoyed that he had.

"Mother said things." His voice was calm, absent his conventional quiver. "Things about Kenneth, about the mayor, about the Braymer family."

"Your mother was a liar, Rich. A manipulator. She was trying to save her own skin."

Richard continued to gaze at Emily, studying her, looking for the slightest break in her demeanor. "I was thinking that if she'd been blackmailing the mayor, why would he interfere with this investigation? Why would he be pressing for her death to be ruled a suicide? I'd think he'd just be glad she was gone, that he'd want to stay separated from any connection to her." Here he paused, leaning closer yet. "That is," he added. "Unless someone else was pulling the strings. Someone still alive to manipulate him."

Emily continued staring forward, not offering Richard the courtesy of eye contact. "She's gone, Rich. Leave it be. You have a company to run now. You should focus on that."

Richard fought the urge to scream at her, but held his temper. Not now. Not here. Later. "I've never wanted to run her company, Em. That's not me. And most of what she did... She was into some areas I just don't want to touch."

Emily angled her head toward Richard, offered a reassuring smile, and slid her palm against his cheek "Don't you worry about that, Rich. I'll take care of everything. You just follow my lead – like a good little rabbit."

GREAT BOOKS

E-BOOKS

AUDIOBOOKS

&

MORE

Visit us today

www.speakingvolumes.us

www.ingramcontent.com/pod-product-compliance
Lightning Source LLC
Chambersburg PA
CBHW050800250626
47155CB00005B/2152